THE SHADOW CLAN SUPREMACY

The Lanterncup series

ISBN 978-0-9964830-2-5

90000

9 780996 483025

Author: Marcus Tay (11 years old)

Printed in the United States of America

@2015 Tay's Imagination World.

ISBN #: 978-0-9964830-2-5

Adoiko — The Northern Hemisphere

Forest of Rampikes

Arctic Reef

Cold Dunes

• Faysie

• Kakutah

• Paya

Shadow Clan Territory

Tropical Fruit Plantation

outstretched Land

Goliather's Lair

Kan • • Cooc
• Toosh

Farmland

• Tache

Kaloocor

Motique

Jungle of Mazes

North Pole

Gulf of Massive Ice Craters

Mt ORSO

Cave

Wall Line

Moor

Tatso

Saik

I.I.I.C.

• Yun

Dop

Underwater Volcanoes

Topwa

• Mooba

Forest of Traps

• Yart

Island of perfection

eeto

Sand Bay

Desert of Longing

Land of Secrets

Plane Wreckage

Known

The Mountain of Day and Night

FFFFF Bistro • Tad

Terp

Grekia Crent

snagids

Lotan

naih

• Cretan

Teen

equator Line

steland

Islandships

idden

scape

k

My Apologies

I'm sorry for making the first book too intense and with too many fatal casualties. But if you prefer that sort of thing, assume that I am just kidding.

I'm sorry for making too many males in the previous book, I will try to make more females in this next edition.

Dedication

To whomever are fans of comedy
and action put together

P.S. Enjoy this one, savor it

Contents:

Prologue: A New Plan

"Did they succeed?" "Yes." "Well, after observing how they took down all those obstacles so easily, I'm profoundly impressed." "Indeed."

The Colonel and His Majesty were back in their little lounge relaxing. A floating hearth turned in circles before both of them. Steam tickled their skin. All was dark around them.

"So, they got the crystal. What's next? Should we just visit them and attack straight-on, or work behind their backs?" His Majesty asked. "I'm guessing option two," the Colonel replied. "We can use other people to fulfill our wishes!" the Colonel exclaimed.

"Oh yeah, but don't you think we are procrastinating by not just sending some of our comrades to steal the crystal from them while they are asleep?" His Majesty inquired. "Well…" the Colonel trailed off. "Don't you think?"

"But they have that metallic-animal creature, and it doesn't need to sleep!" the Colonel brought up apprehensively. "It's a he," His Majesty pointed out. "Oh whatever, but believe me, that creature is extremely vicious!" the Colonel added. "He doesn't look like it," His Majesty responded.

"Argh, we have to get him away from them, though," the Colonel said. "But how?" His Majesty asked, partly to himself. There was a period of silence.

Suddenly, the Colonel looked up at His Majesty and grinned. "I do have an idea, but the question is, do you deserve to listen to it?" "Anyway, I command you to tell me!" His Majesty demanded, suddenly interested and curious.

The Colonel bent his head closer. "You know Shadow Clan, right?" he questioned. "Do you mean the creatures who live on the far-east-most continent? Where lies their territory?" His Majesty inquired.

"Yes," the Colonel paused, "but this time, we're not going to use human beings, Shadow Clan citizens are our next pawns," he explained. "Then how?" His Majesty asked curiously. "Let me tell you," the Colonel put his hand up.

"We will become newspaper writers!" he exclaimed exuberantly. "What? Excuse me?"

"Yeah, because, you see, Shadow Clan loves to keep in touch with mankind's society. They even have careers for citizens who don't have degrees including fishing-out interesting news that they Shadow-Travel back to print. It's a fairly easy job," the Colonel summarized.

"But how are we going to catch their attention?" His Majesty considered. The Colonel lifted his head, almost abruptly, and spoke, "We can put up AD signs at the nearest city, Kakutah." "How many?" "Countless!" the Colonel replied automatically.

"I still don't get it, what are we going to write about?" His Majesty wondered. "About how much mankind resents Shadow Clan. We are going to pretend that we are average newspaper writers and set a hatred field between both races," the Colonel explained.

"What an impeccable idea! But how is this supposed to support us into getting the crystal?" His Majesty inquired. The Colonel looked sideways and thought for a moment, and then he glanced back. "As Shadow Clan can no more bear their anguish, they will start attacking nearby human-inhabited areas," he said.

"That metallic-animal of Ian's, will go back to try to keep the ruckus at bay. In the meantime, we will snatch that Shadow-Talk of theirs and incinerate it in the realm of The Haunter, where there's nothing but nothing!" the Colonel stood up and spread his arms.

"Are you sure the metallic-animal won't sense it being destroyed?" His Majesty questioned. "Of course!" the Colonel answered.

"There's still one problem, or at least I think so," His Majesty announced apprehensively, "if we make Shadow Clan abhor humans, how are *we* going to convince them to become our allies?"

"Isn't that the point? I came up with this plan so we can steal the crystal under their pesky noses. And therefore, take the object to the Shadow Clan territory and present it to the king," the Colonel breathed heavily. His Majesty's face revealed a contrite expression. "You sure they won't have our heads?" His Majesty questioned.

"Of course not! The reason this archaic piece of matter exists, is because it symbolizes friendship, and *they* know that," the Colonel started.

"So if we bring them the crystal, there is no doubt that Shadow Clan will join forces with us, will be by our side in any type of conflict for as long mankind walks on earth," the Colonel elaborated, his voice cracking. "Wonderful!" His Majesty answered.

One: The Solving of a Code

Why did it have to start like this? Why did it come so near to another plane? Was it going to destroy the plane with a good chance of killing every passenger onboard too? Did the creature have any link to The Haunter? Ian thought rapidly.

Every limb of Ian's body seemed as if each one became autonomous. They made movements that Ian's own mind didn't even recognize for a tedious four seconds.

He stared blankly at the creature's moldy carapace. Ian was quite astounded that The Snamel had swam an endless amount of miles to greet them. Or was it for another purpose?

Ian tried to calm himself, to keep his composure, his equanimity, and to not freak out. He abruptly decided to see how things were going in the cockpit.

Ian took one quick final glance at the sea, but what he saw made his eyes bulge: a pair of maroon eyes looking cross-eyed right through the window into the seat where he was. Ian gulped, and his muscles tightened.

People all around were scratching their heads because the plane stopped moving in midair. Ian knew why; The Snamel took a hold of the plane, literally.

Ian bit his lower lip with his front-upper-tooth. He saw that a claw was raised and shut his eyes right away. Ian stood transfixed for three seconds until taking a glimpse and finding a surprise.

The Snamel had its palm up, and in it were six little eggs with seaweed strips wrapped around them. So, Ian thought, The Snamel was a she. What a discovery!

The Snamel settled the six unhatched eggs on her flat and smooth head and lifted her claw once again. Ian braced for the worse.

But instead, she used one of her nails and scratched a number on the window. Ian saw that it was the number 7209, with a double line under the first digit, the number seven. Why did she write that?

Ian put up his hand to give an 'I need some time to think' gesture and pondered hard. What was she referring to? What is the relationship from six unhatched eggs to the number 7209 and a double line under the left-most digit? Ian thought of many possibilities.

But a couple times, he fell out of track, including: Where in the world did The Snamel learn numbers?? Was she once a human?? Then Ian thought of Lady Harsh, a she-villain he met days ago, but shook her image out of his head before it became too strong to resist.

If I couldn't get the answer, would I, my friends, and the entire plane be doomed? Ian thought, as The Snamel waited sort-of patiently and very glumly. He knew many pairs of eyes were fixed on him, as if he was their only hope.

"Ian, Ian?" Drake called silently. Drake was Ian's best friend from school who had agreed to go on a quest with him, a friend-girl of theirs, and their school janitor to pretty much steal a priceless crystal from the depths of the tallest point in the world. He had gotten a glade as a weapon and almost died from being shot by a revolver.

Ian didn't dare move a muscle. "I have a feeling those eggs are 'artificial', you see what I mean?" Drake wondered. Ian opened, but shut his mouth almost immediately, biting his tongue.

Ian shuddered, "Not the time." "It's ok, please just answer me," Drake pleaded. "Fine! You think," Ian took a deep, deep breath, "that the eggs are fake?" he whispered, trying to keep his pace not too fast and not too slow. "Yes! And I do see that you are attempting to figure out what THAT monster is trying to tell you," Drake considered.

The Snamel roared, shaking the plane while doing it. "I don't think she likes being called a monster. If that is so, she must be a marvelous mouth-reader," Alexis squeaked. "Agreed," Drake said silently.

Alexis was both Ian and Drake's friend who is always apprehensive about the future, I mean, seconds into it. A few days ago, she had realized that she could talk to living animals. Both of her friend-boys are very enthusiastic about her.

Anyway....

Ian glanced at the plastic window, his teeth biting down on the inside of his cheek. He saw that The Snamel lifted both her claws and stretched them like how a gecko would. Ian understood that she was about to do a countdown. Ian felt sick, really sick. Then he thought of it.

"Wait!" Ian took his exquisite gadget, the Wrist Striker 280 from out of thin air and used it to smash the plastic of the window into shards. He could get stuff out of thin air because they made a friend with this male named Flix who is of a unique race named Shadow Clan, and he could toss things out of the void to humans.

"Hey, I understand now! You double-underlined the first digit because it is the number of years it takes until your eggs hatch, because it is crucial. While that is that, the number 209 is how long humans shouldn't cross the sea because you don't want your kids to be harmed and annoyed until they grow out of their childhood. Am I right? Or am I not??" Ian cried.

"Wow, they have long lives before becoming adolescents!" Alexis spoke in Drake's ear. "Oh yeah," Drake replied, a tad soft. Ian, however, didn't turn around to make a response, for it seemed to him unnecessary at the moment.

Ian arched his eyebrow at The Snamel. She nodded half-heartedly, rolled her eyes, and....smirked. Why did she smirk? Ian thought.

He suddenly went SMACK on the hard-carpet floor and went sliding down the aisle to the back. Ian attempted to grab a hold of something, but he just couldn't.

He also saw that a few others including Joe, who was Ian and his friends' school janitor that later became their chaperone in their quest to get a crystal also went sliding down above him. Ian saw the undersides of somebody's boots. Ian knew The Snamel had just brandished the plane as if it was a toy, and tilted it to a cockpit-up position.

Then, there was a piercing groan, and the plane plummeted. Ian knew any moment, they would plunge into the sea, the windows would shatter, and they would be left to try to swim back to shore, how unfortunate!

As Ian started sliding towards the front this time, he glanced out a different side window and saw that the sea was about to swallow them. But then he felt the plane rise vertically and joy entered his soul. Ian etched a grin.

He got up and ran to the cockpit, bumping into Joe. "Man, that was sure a hit!" he exclaimed. "What are you up to now?" Joe inquired, his countenance suddenly serious.

"Getting a pack of cashews," Ian lied. "Well," Joe chuckled, "go for it!" Joe turned sideways to let Ian wisp pass. Joe was one of the kind that recovered from shock really quickly.

Ian sprinted instead of running, for he wanted to avoid anonymous people that wanted to stop and ask him questions. After 25-30 seconds, he finally made it to the little control-compartment pilots took most of their time in.

Right in front of Ian, were buttons, levers, knobs, speakers, and gear sticks that made the room look very complex and sophisticated. Ian wondered how long people who were seeking for a pilot's degree needed to attend college for. He stared, awestruck, at the three different control panels that occupied space below the window that was shaped like the top-half of a hexagon. Ian got snapped out of it after a second or two.

"Who are YOU? What are you DOING here?" questioned a man in a white shirt and black long pants who got up from his chair on the right.

"Uh—you are the pilot, right?" Ian guessed and assumed. "NO! Have you ever heard of co-pilots?" the man asked. "Y-y-yes!" Ian answered. Wow, the guy sure was dyspeptic.

He had cheeks that drooped and touched his chin, making his mouth resemble the shape of a rectangle, angry green eyes, and lines on his forehead. He looked about 55-60.

"So, where's the main…." Ian didn't have to finish. The leather chair on the left squealed, and a person said, "Hey, Lance, can you do the driving for now?" His colleague grunted and went to take the wheel.

A gentleman with a kinder face stood up and strode over to Ian. "Nice to meet you, what's your name?" he inquired. Ian considered on this. He always knew people who asked him his name first, but never vice-versa.

"Oh! I'm Ian." "Ian, eh?" "Yeah!" "So, tell me, why are you here?" the dude asked. "To get a clear picture of what happened," Ian blurted. "Sure!" the dude replied.

"What occurred was when that sea thingamajig was going to give us a blow, two jets behind us flew out of nowhere and shot volley after volley of rockets at it," the guy explained. "It's a she!" Ian interrupted. "Oh, ok."

"But, how did whoever was on land know what was coming for this plane?" Ian inquired. "We contacted the control tower," the guy responded, nonchalantly. "Oh yeah, I didn't think of that."

Ian abruptly thanked the pilot for informing him, and walked into the nearest lavatory. He locked the thin door so it read 'occupied' and thrust out his Shadow-Talk device.

It was a tad smaller than the main body of your hand, and it looked like a walkie-talkie, but with yellow neon lines traced around the edge. Instead of having an antennae protruding from the top, there was a glossy hand with a wavy pattern on it.

"Flix, Flix," Ian spoke into the speaker. In a split second, a figure materialized in front of him. Flix was skinny and had a body made of iron. He had white dots as eyes and three hands, four fingers each, crammed at the end of a reptile-like tail. Flix appeared to be very flamboyant because of sets and pairs of blue lines that ran everywhere on him.

"Hello, we speak again," he said. Ian was dying to ask Flix a question that gnawed at himself.

"Hey, for the past hour or so, I was thinking of," Ian paused, Flix gave him a nod to reassure him to keep going, "when we get to Terp, why don't we just take another plane that can fly to the closest city we can get to Shadow Clan?? Do you think I'm a genius or what??"

Flix just puffed air, which, to humans, is a sigh. He took out his Shadow-Map and tapped it, so it would show Adolko, and it did. Flix took his pointer finger and settled it on the center.

"This continent right here, the one with our world capital, Tarso, on it, doesn't allow planes to fly over itself," Flix explained. "But we can still board a plane that flies next to the perimeter, right?" Ian inquired. "Nope!" Flix replied. "What?"

"Yes, this concerns with the law. It is because no one is allowed to drive any air vehicle inside a 68-mile radius from the perimeter, which is just below that cove right there." Flix traced his finger north to where there was a little dent in the land. "So our only remedy is to travel south by foot and go the long way," Flix concluded. Ian groaned.

"I don't get it, tell me more," Ian demanded. "Fine. The reason why, is because the High-Government fears that terrorists from Dop would smuggle atomic bombs into passenger planes and drop them," Flix said. "Oh!" Ian blurted abruptly. "Yup!"

"Well, I should be going, I need to visit my homeland," Flix told Ian. "Sure, but can I call you anytime?" Ian asked. Flix eyed him steadily. "Yes, you are permitted to!" Flix answered. And with that, he wisped into the void.

Ian exited the lavatory and bumped into Jarret, who was one of his mom's side cousins. Everyone had thought Jarret had died after plunging into a river, but he said he woke up in a public restroom and felt a strong desire to go to where Ian was heading. They both first met on a plane but didn't know each other. It was not unto they got to their destination, and in a cave there, realized who each other was. Ian had wept tears of joy and hugged Jarret for minutes.

"Hey, you ok? No injuries, right?" Ian asked in a somewhat concerned tone. Jarret glared at him. "Of course not! How else did you think I survived the first plane attack from The Snamel?" Jarret said and asked.

"But you were crying!" Ian chuckled. "No—fine, but I was only three, do you remember that I became seven again after glancing at you through the crystal??" "Yeah, but I liked it when you were a toddler!" Ian teased.

"Oh, really, huh, you want me to throw a punch at you right now, in front of all these people?" Jarret readied his fist. "Nah, I don't feel like it," Ian responded from the corner of his mouth.

He grinned, made a fake yawn, and switched angles to walk back to where he sat.

On his way back, Ian saw Drake and Alexis chatting. He stopped at their row and they tucked in their legs to let him pass.

Before taking a seat, Ian faced Joe, who was a row behind him, and asked for the time. Joe said 8:50 pm.

Ian didn't want to stay another night in a hotel after what happened to the previous one they were in, but he knew if they were going to, three rooms with two king-sized beds each would be comforting.

They could sleep in their tents for that night, but Ian was too lazy to stretch his out. He also doubted that even half of his team would vote to sleep in the outdoors because of interesting recent news on TV telling the public about them with a crystal cuddled in their arms. At least there was a better chance of not getting robbed because they were in a building, Ian hoped.

Two: The Never-Seen Animals

The plane touched-down on the runway, and Ian's eyes flew open. It wasn't the rumbling that woke him, but instead, he had felt a freezing hand grip his left shoulder.

Ian glanced back and only saw Jarret, who sat next to Joe's seat. "Cuz, your hand is really cold," Ian pointed out. "No…it's warm, what do you mean?" Jarret questioned, perplexed.

"Didn't you wake me up by putting your hand on my….?" Ian cut short because there was no hint in Jarret's countenance that he had done it. "What? You must have been half-asleep!" Jarret exclaimed.

"Why would I wake you up in your deep sleep before the plane even stops moving?" he added. "Well…" Ian always talked-back like that even though he would not continue. "Give me a break!" Jarret responded adamantly.

Ian shrugged and turned towards his two best friends. Unfortunately, they were snoring like barn animals, so Ian couldn't confide with them about what Flix told him.

It wasn't at all good news, but it was worthy enough to be acknowledged.

The plane finally came to a halt and people started getting up and taking their luggage from the storages above their seats.

Ian shook Drake up, and during the process, Alexis awoke as well.

Ian spotted Joe jostling other passengers to try to get to them. He stumbled over random people's legs and had to crawl to them the last few feet. Joe looked injured.

"Anything went wrong?" Drake inquired. Joe looked both relieved and uncomfortable. "Yes, I'm listening," Ian mumbled as he reached for his duffel bag. Joe's lips tensed. "If you don't want to tell us, it's ok," Alexis assured him.

"Fine, I went to the lavatory in the back, I had constipation, and was in there for forty-some minutes. When I was done, I accidentally banged my knee into the dustbin. Then, out came a brown rat that threw itself at the back of my right thigh, and there…it bit me!" Joe blurted vigorously and sheepishly.

Ian kept his lips as tight as ever to prevent breaking into hysteric laughter. Drake narrowed his at-first grin to a frown. Alexis did nothing. Jarret settled both of his hands on his cheeks and applied pressure (his extraordinary technique).

But at that moment, a flight-attendant's voice spoke, "We will now start letting everyone off. Please remember to take all belongings. And thank you for riding on WhiteWind-Winners!"

"Also, don't forget our special 65% percent off during Thanksgiving weekend. Hope to see you all soon! I hope you lot remembered to fill in your immigrating cards."

Everyone went off the plane and through a long tunnel.

Ian and his friends appeared at Gate 28 and Joe checked his watch. "It is almost half-past midnight!" he exclaimed. And sure enough, nothing beyond the airport's property and ground could be seen, only sparkling lights in the distance.

"Ok, now, we need to know how to get out of here," Jarret groaned. "And then where we are going to spend the night," Alexis added. "Maybe we should ask someone for directions to get of this terminal first," Ian suggested.

Drake was the first one that spotted somebody who seemed free for help.

It was this figure in a brown hat with dangling fringes and an enormous brochure that covered most of him. It wore a very fluffy dark-blue coat that was the same color as the floor.

Joe strode over to the figure. "Um, uh," he started, "do you know the way out of here?" It ignored him. "I was saying…! Joe snapped, and tore the brochure from his meaty hands.

At first sight of the figure, Ian couldn't inhale nor exhale. Drake had a confused look. Joe ran back and hid behind Alexis. What a coward! The creature hopped, and for that split second, they took-in what was really in front of them.

The figure wasn't a human at all, it was a creature that Ian had never learned about in his school. It had a panda's head, a seahorse's tail, and a fat seahorse's body and limbs with white fur on the rough skin. All in all, it resembled ¼ panda, ¼ polar bear, and ½ seahorse.

Then when it hit the floor again, its fur turned dark-blue. "What the…" Jarret squeaked. "It's part seahorse. Whatever a seahorse touches, its body turns to the color that specific object has to camouflage and hide from prey," Alexis explained nonchalantly.

"Can you speak English?" Drake asked curiously. "Good question," Alexis agreed. Ian watched the creature shake his head. "Do you know how to listen to…?" Ian started. The animal nodded this time.

"So it knows how to listen to English, not speak it," Alexis confirmed, tugging at her sleeve to try to get Joe lose his grip. "Seems like it," Ian whistled in an upright tone. Drake looked at him and said, "I agree."

"So, um, this might be rude, but, what are you?" Drake inquired as he fidgeted. "Drake!" Alexis yelled, not too loud. "Give him a notepad and a pen," Ian suggested. "Are you sure it knows how to write?" Jarret questioned. "No," Ian replied smoothly.

Joe was the first to act. He swiftly dug in his personal duffel bag and brought out the items. Then, Joe offered it to the creature with trembling hands.

It took the pile, and during the process, tickled a section of Joe's hand with its polar bear fur. Joe howled and sprinted to the restrooms, clutching his hand like it had just been scared by ticks.

The creature snorted several times as it wrote whatever it intended to. After it was done, it handed the notepad back to Ian. This was what they read:

Race: Moygeri   Gender: Female

Name: Baily

"A Moygeri? What is that??" Drake wondered, his spit flying onto the lined-paper. "You know, sometimes stuff don't make much sense in life," Ian considered thoughtfully. "It's funny," he added. "Don't you think?"

"Never mind you two," Alexis muttered. "I'm very much surprised it's a she!" Jarret exclaimed, astonished. "Hey, I was about to say that!" Alexis complained and argued.

Ian saw Joe limp towards them and blowing air like he had just gone through a tantrum. "Hey, show me the piece of paper," Joe ordered.

He stared at it for several seconds before nodding his approval.

Then Joe turned to address Baily the Moygeri. "So...can you teach us the way out of here? Out of this place, this plane-station?"

Joe hesitated and spoke in Ian's ear, "Wait, does she actually know English?" "Yeah, she just can't speak it, but can listen, read, and write with the language," Ian muttered. "Oh," Joe answered.

So they trudged on and out the entire airport. Then they took a heavily-packed subway to uptown Terp.

While they were on the metro, Ian asked, "So…Baily, are there anyone else of your kind?" Just then, the doors slid open, and Baily took her hand and gestured towards the city outside.

Ian fast-walked out, not even aware of the gap under him. He hurried to the railing.

Ian looked down from the high-overpass the subway was on, and sure enough, Moygeri clogged the streets, each changing color from time to time.

"There are a few humans, but not many," Jarret started pointing several out. "Oh yeah," Ian replied, his eyes following where Jarret's finger went. "I hope the humans feel okay as in the minority," Alexis said. "Are you kidding me? I love this city!" Drake yelled, grinning.

"Yo, let's go down," cried Joe, who stood next to an escalator. Together, they hurried to catch-up and descended into a narrow alley.

"So, uh, Baily, where do people spend their nights in this city?" Ian inquired. Baily made a 'don't know' gesture. She quickly pointed at herself and made a thumbs-up. "Uh what do you mean?" Drake interrupted. "I think…" Alexis started.

Suddenly, Baily grabbed the top of Ian's left ear and put her mouth to it. "What are you, what?" Joe screamed, dropping his own duffel bag, ready to tackle Baily the Moygeri. Jarret averted his eyes so he wouldn't witness what was the result. Drake and Alexis both seemed to forget how to act.

All Ian heard was "looahlooahlooahlooah."

Three: The Interview

Ian awoke, his eyes closed, and his head drooped. The sound Baily the Moygeri made into him was still echoing in his ear.

He felt that he was in a chair made of some sort of metal, and slowly powered-on his sense of sight. At first glance, Ian couldn't see anyone.

Ian realized that he couldn't move his feet nor his hands. His wrist and ankles were strapped onto four glossy surfaces of silver with leather belts. Was this an electric chair? Ian's first thought was. His eyes started wandering about the room.

High-tech cameras were all over the ceiling and positioned so that the lenses faced towards Ian.

But the thing that really freaked him out was a gargantuan video-taper with buttons on its side that hung 3-5 feet from his forehead. Ian gulped, wondering if he was on international TV.

The wall had a pattern of striped-colors: orange, pink, dark-green; orange, pink, dark-green.

Then suddenly, a voice higher than a soprano spoke, "Are you awake yet?" Ian poked his head around to try to find the source. Finally, a lady with short-silver-dyed hair appeared around the corner of a hallway on the right, which was in front of Ian.

A thought rushed into Ian's mind, and he accidentally put it into words, creating a question. It was, "Is your name, or surname, for instance, Lady H?" Ian blurted. A split-second later, Ian totally regret what he, himself, said.

"Oh!" the woman exclaimed, a tad confused. "Surely not, I'm…" she stopped short. "Oh whatever," she continued abruptly, "it's none of your business anyway, let's just get back to what's necessary." "Ok, all right," Ian responded reluctantly.

"So…where did I left off…aha, you are about to be on the Abnormal Characters' Secrets Revealed Channel, often known as the ACSRC," the lady spoke, her voice getting more and more high-pitched.

"Over 20 million watch our reports ever day! Therefore, while I banter with you, please cooperate, and give the entire audience of anonymous people an authentic smile! The show will start in four minutes or so."

Ian grimaced. He felt very apprehensive, and in that case, more than on a stage although there weren't any real people present in the room.

"Ok, please, but can you elaborate?" Ian inquired, his heart pounding. "Too late," she took a seat across Ian on a one-person-couch. "That wasn't four minutes!" Ian blurted abruptly. "And you're on!" the lady whinnied.

"Hello! And good early-morning! Welcome to our awards-winning ACSRC on television and smart phones." The lady took a deep breath.

"Today, we will be learning about this fantastic youngster," she presented Ian with her hand, "who is known to have exploded one flying beast and trapped the other in a priceless crystal from out of midair," she licked her bottom teeth greedily. "They are dragons!" Ian interrupted, not knowing that he wasn't allowed to speak yet.

"One gray, another yellow, and…" Ian shut him mouth instantly because the lady gave him a message to stop by taking her pointer finger, putting it with her thumb, and drawing an invisible line in thin air, which clearly meant 'shut up'.

"So, I think our person of the day doesn't really understand the basics when he is on TV with others, but anyway, we shall proceed to the questioning. I hope you all would learn something new and essential," she winked and smiled, then turned to Ian.

"Well, keeping in mind that you participated in a skirmish with those crafty dragons, I have acquired knowledge that a cryptic sea creature actually communicated with you through numbers," the lady said spookily.

Ian opened his mouth several inches wide, and the lady assured him to reply. Ian decided to make the best of his once-in-a-lifetime situation.

A serious and humorous answer would be excellent at the moment, Ian thought, but both attributes just didn't solve the puzzle for a response because they were opposites. It indeed was hard to make-up a comment in no more than a snap.

"Yes, miss, I agree, the sea monster was eccentric, and acknowledging how she knew numbers is really brain-shaking indeed," Ian gave his best shot.

"A she?" the lady cried, taking a quick note on her pamphlet. "Apparently," Ian answered nonchalantly. "Very surprising indeed," he added.

"Then, how come the sea-thing was focused on you the entire time it was there, and not anyone else? Do you happen to have a theory?" Ian scratched the side of his head for a moment. "Maybe because it remembered me from at the first plane-attack I survived," Ian wondered and shrugged.

"Then is there anything about this monster that is empirical?" "Yeah, how it looks like," Ian replied smoothly. "Oh well, we don't have much time for elaboration of the creature's appearance, so let us move on." The lady grunted unhappily and changed topic.

"I also heard that you and several buddies went to prison for half-a-day," she considered.

"Do we have to discuss this?" Ian muttered, barely moving his mouth. "Of course! Now, how did you feel about prison? Please give full detail."

"I'm sorry, but, can we cancel this interview right now?" Ian asked stubbornly, knowing the possibility that the lady was up to something. "But that would be unfortunate!"

"Come on," Ian pleaded boldly, not afraid of what the public, the whole-wide world, would think of him anymore. He didn't care, but just wanted to leave immediately.

"Fine!" she hopped up, and cracked the screen of the gargantuan video-taper with her foot.

Ian took a run for it as the woman screamed colorfully, and also yelling, "You cannot and will not escape by foot! My employees are now running up the stairs to catch you! Hand over the crystal, and you shall be 'let-go' silently.

He sprinted down the left hallway. Ian stopped at one intersection and ran right, through a different corridor, and then left again, where he saw a door that led outside into the platform on top of the building.

Ian ran towards it, but stopped a few feet away because something caught his eye.

He glanced right, and to his gratefulness, saw his two best friends, Joe, and Jarret, all tied-up with masking tape over their mouths. Ian hurried in and untangled the ropes. "Hurry, we have to leave," he cried, and they obeyed.

Together, Ian and his friends barged out into the cool air of dawn, and spotted a helicopter thirty feet in front of them.

"Joe! Can you fly that?" Ian yelled and pointed towards the air vehicle. "Over all the subjects at school I fail at, driving any vehicle is my destiny," Joe responded sincerely.

When at last they made it, each climbed aboard rather clumsily and quickly fastened their seat-belts.

All around them were bullet-proof vests on hangers and night-vision goggles dangling from the ceiling. They were in a military helicopter!! What was it doing here?

Joe worked his way to the mini-cockpit and his hands went flying everywhere on the single control panel.

The helicopter lifted-off ground, and for several seconds, seemed as if it was suspended in midair as Joe tinkered with the buttons in the front.

Ian saw people in blue uniforms emerge from a bumpy-black surfaced door they ran out of. But then…the helicopter…ascended into the ethereal sky of dawn.

Four: Attacked in Midair

Not only were there humans aboard—the leather flap went up, and two Moygeri heads popped out of Alexis' duffel bag that was carried like a 'backpack' (on her back) hanging loosely on one shoulder.

The curious creatures doubled-over and crawled down onto the floor.

"Aren't they fabulous?" Alexis cried, staring at the two little critters, which were only one and a half feet tall. "Wait, let me confirm, they're little kids, right?" Jarret questioned. "Well, yeah!" Alexis corroborated sternly.

But as Ian watched the entire time, excitement didn't overcome him. Instead, he felt outrageous and disrespected. Ian began to feel very irritated and annoyed.

And somehow, Ian was uncomfortable that Moygeri were accompanying them on this perilous trip. Maybe because they looked *so* different and strange, and peculiar.

Anyway, he felt that Alexis was being preposterous by bringing repulsive creatures that they hardly know with them, and that she didn't ask Ian permission before. Ian had quite enough.

"Anything wrong?" Alexis inquired worriedly, looking at him like she was trying to read his thoughts. "Yes! I do!" Ian gave a straightforward response, his eyebrows curled.

"Calm down, why are you yelling at Alexis?" Drake inquired, moving in front of her. "Get…out…of…the…way!" Alexis yanked Drake's elbow away. "Hey! I was trying to protect you from *him,* he pointed at Ian, his nail digging into the space between Ian's eyes. "Well, you two are driving me nuts!" Alexis screamed.

"What is it with these boys in front of me?" she switched-gears, glancing out the arch-shaped window. "Why can't they keep their equanimity for long stretches of time?" she muttered to herself.

Alexis started to seem to be telling the sky outside to help her go someplace else where she would kind different friends that were female and forget her old ones (Drake and Ian).

Ian knew that she had always complained to the head counselor of their school that all her girl-classmates were somewhat 'evil' according to Alexis. Ian never understood what that meant.

"Hey, Ian! Why did you make her sad?" Drake glared at him, demanding a reply. "I didn't…" "Don't lie to me that you didn't know it was hurtful," Drake snapped. "I knew Josh should have been your best…" "STOP! Don't talk me anymore!" Ian screamed, tears spilling out.

"Everything all right?" Joe called from behind the closed door in the front, his voice was muffled, but the words could still be distinguished.

"It's good, they are just rapping without rhythm!" Jarret lied, who seemed a big fan of their angry dispute, and didn't want it to end. He pounded his fist on the palm of his other hand, demanding more.

Ian wasn't in a hurry to adjourn, and went in with another phrase. "I wish you were never b-b," Ian couldn't finish, why would he be saying this to old Drake, whom had been his best friend for five years?

Ian's lips contracted into a serious smile, and built-up the urge to say, "I'm sorry, gentleman." Drake, however did not respond, but instead, had his own mouth ajar, lifting one eyebrow. "Really?" "Yes," Ian substantiated.

Jarret looked haggard and not as bright as before, but he was slightly okay.

After more than ten seconds of body language, the three of them silently decided to keep Alexis alone for a while as they held a private 'boy talk' in the corner.

"So, may somebody tell me why that…that Moygeri," Ian stuttered, "made noises directly into my ear?" he finished awkwardly. "We did find out that Moygeri made sounds into each other's ears to fall asleep," Jarret piped up. "You are telling me that they don't care about rain, that they don't have homes?" Ian inquired. "Apparently," Drake responded.

"We also did learn that they never spend time in human stores and restaurants because they are afraid of air-conditioning." "Then where would they get their food?" Ian asked. "Shops and catering places their own kind open-up, obviously," Drake interrupted.

"Now tell us, what happened to you before you found us in an unlocked room?" Jarret inquired. "I got interviewed," Ian replied nonchalantly. "What?" Drake feigned surprise.

"Let me ask you guys, what happened after I fell into deep sleep?" Ian questioned. "Oh, that creature is like an athletic sloth that is faster than a man. We fell asleep too!" Drake sighed. "And then, the next thing we knew, was, getting dragged into the room you found us in," Jarret cried.

"So it was all certainly planned," Ian muttered. "Excuse me?" Drake and Jarret said at the same time. "That woman that began a one-on-one interview with me wanted the crystal. She must've not know Joe had it connected to his staff…where are your weapons?"

Ian jumped up in alarm. "Don't worry, Joe's staff is perfectly safe in his duffel bag so as mines. We saw them just sitting there outside the door and snatched them," Drake said.

"But I have no idea why they didn't remove my glade and…" Drake took a glimpse into the void.

"Maybe they were afraid an explosive was hidden in the bags…or," Ian puffed-up his cheeks as they looked at him, calculating, "hey, have you ever heard of shoe and underwear bombs?" They continued to stare at him with eyes that didn't dare to blink. "Just a thought," Ian shrugged. He abruptly changed topic.

"Um, about this whole Moygeri coming with us on a quest thing, I am not liking it. You might as well tell me their names, and how you met them," Ian whispered.

"Oh, that's easy, those two critters appeared, and Baily said something about them guiding us along our trip and that's when I passed-out," Jarret said and turned to Drake, "did you hear anything more, another phrase?" he asked hopefully. "Nope!" Drake blurted. Jarret groaned.

"And...the smaller one is male, named Blake, the larger one, female, called Batelo," Drake vigorously spoke.

"These...these two...two younglings are ordered to do what? To escort us? To teach us the way? We have maps, what's the point? Were they really sent to look after us? I don't think so!" Ian exclaimed sufficiently.

Suddenly, everything went white. We're in a cloud right now," Alexis' voice came, and she stood up. Ian and Drake both wisped around at the same time.

"My stress has alleviated, I feel better," Alexis said, but Ian could still hear that she had a melancholy voice. "Seriously, be honest, you do?" Drake inquired. "Yeah," she replied back, saying it like a newcomer and just-met classmate.

Ian glanced at Jarret, who was tapping his foot on the ground. Ian knew he was eavesdropping.

Suddenly, the plane started careening. Ian could have slipped if it wasn't for the rough floor.

Then, this happened. The sound of a rotor became very audible over the howling wind, and then FONG, FONG, FONG, WEESH.

Bits of titanium and aluminum flew all over the place, and this time, Ian had no choice but to fall onto the floor and cover his eyes.

When he opened them, a gap was formed right under a circular window next to the wide 'troop deploy' area of the military helicopter.

Ian heard Joe grunting and turned around to see Drake hurt, a cut where his funny-bone was, his arm falling to the ground. Alexis scrambled over to check the wound.

Ian lifted one knee to attempt to get closer to Drake, but after half-a-sec, Ian glanced outdoors and with a jolt of shock, saw a figure with a green vest, green long pants, and goggles that covered his red-blank eyes.

It was a creature called Zhowltagook, who was a Zartee. He flew at the opened and narrow entrance of their helicopter.

The creature looked different from before, because this time, he had visible fish gills inside his cheeks that glowed bright-pinkish-brown, and, was wearing gloves that could stick to anything except air. A rope was tied to him at his back.

Ian blinked several times before glancing wherever he could to see the outdoors with tearful eyes. Sure enough, Zartees swung at them from the sides, as far as Ian knew. They were unusually surrounded (in the sky). Not a good sign.

Ian couldn't consider any positive outcomes at the moment. He did know that there were slim ones, but barely any. Ian didn't even want to think of the worst possibilities, for they will hinder his awareness of what's present.

Then, a knife poked inside, through the chassis, and Alexis was just a couple feet away from it, muttering things to Drake, who sat on the floor, his lips bent.

"Look out!" Ian bellowed, jutting his finger behind her. "Wait, what?" she looked up, baffled.

Drake acted before Ian did. He put his left leg next to her heels to stop her from going backwards if she wanted to, and then gave her a tug forward. Alexis stumbled, and came to a halt. Now, they had far-worse things to worry about.

Wind rushed into the compartment. A Zartee did a front-flip and landed inside. He smiled sardonically. "Well, well, well, it is surely time for close-combat fighting! Let us get started," he exclaimed, twirling his knife on his index finger.

Ian always thought that his Wrist Striker 280 was more of a long-distance-usable gadget, but he proved it wrong. Ian leaped at the Zartee and bashed him in the gut.

For two seconds, the Zartee seemed resilient to fight-back. But he lose his poise almost suddenly and plunged backwards, as straight as a surfboard, down where he entered from.

After that heroic act, Ian felt unexpectedly powerful. His friends were glaring at him, their eyebrows arched. Ian then cried, "Boo-yah! Wasn't that awesome?" he inquired. But then, he was knocked off his feet as usual.

"Don't celebrate too quickly," came the voice of dear-old Zhowltagook.

"Our law is that, if you murder one of us…" "He fell, he wasn't…" Drake complained. "Shut up!" Zhowltagook hissed. Ian mouthed 'nice try' at Drake anyway. "Your life will and shall be taken immediately by one of his friends, that is me in this case," he pointed his thumb at himself.

"That is great!" Alexis cried sarcastically. "What? Repeat what you said," Zhowltagook ordered. Ian side-stepped, creeping up behind him, ready to give a shove. Ian grinned and thought, what if he didn't even know what sarcasm was?

"Tell me!" Zhowltagook begged. "I wish to," Alexis shrugged, "but it will embarrass you in front of these…humans!" "Please!" he pleaded. "Oh fine, now listen," Alexis started.

"You are just *so* charmingly handsome!" Alexis lied and said slowly, pronouncing every syllable with clarity and shaking her head affectionately.

As she started saying "hand", Ian pushed the dreamy-expression Zhowltagook off balance, and he too went flying into the clouds through the broken chassis. His scream could be barely heard.

And then…the helicopter was descending rapidly. Joe appeared, coughing, smoke coming out of the mini-cockpit. "Are you ok?" Drake hurried to support him. Joe put a hand up as substitute of his mouth to say 'I'm perfectly fine' even though he really wasn't.

The air vehicle tilted and jerked from right to left, right to left. They had to escape the situation, but how?

"Ian, Drake, Joe," cried Alexis, "we need to go sky-diving!" Drake and Joe both nodded their heads without second thought, but Ian gritted his teeth with reluctance.

"But..." "We have to, there's no other option!" Alexis yelled.

Ian quickly nodded his approval, still a tad afraid and discouraged. What if he landed in a crocodile swamp?

They tore equipment off hooks and strapped what was needed on themselves. One-by-one they jumped. Ian was second-to-last. Joe was last.

Ian Lanterncup was never a fan of heights. Seeing that the ground keeps drawing nearer him was really heart-wrenching. And evidence of this is his screaming.

"Ian! Open your parachute!" Joe cried from above. He heard Drake bellow the same thing too, but from below.

Ian's hands were super-glued to his hips, but he managed to do what he needed to do in less than a second and a half. In the next split-second, a large dome thingamajig shaded him from the morning sunlight, and then he was on earth again. Did he still know to walk? He hoped so!

"So…Joe, why was it going-down?" Alexis asked. "Oh! I think they sliced the mast of the main rotor in half," Joe said. "You mean they took-off that propeller-like thing on the top?" Drake asked. "Yeah," Joe answered.

"The best things is…we escaped serious trouble as a team!" Jarret exclaimed, then his grin faded.

"Anybody agree? Anyone?" Jarret inquired. Only the two Moygeri that clung onto Alexis' back the whole time they were in the air shot their arms up as quick as fireworks.

Jarret just glanced aside, maybe because he was rather disappointed that he only got two replies from un-human animals.

"All right," Joe started, "we need to get to the nearest city." "Yes!" Ian cried out, without double-checking what he was going to say.

Five: The Permanently-Injured People

They trudged for half-an-hour on a dirt-road that might have once been for traders to walk on, until finally stopping to take a break.

Drake poured the remaining water in his canteen on his hair while Alexis drank her one-liter water from her thermos in only seven gulps and one sip. Joe struggled to twist-open the cap on his plastic bottle. Ian, unfortunately, had to share his precious water with Jarret since he was his cousin. And the two Moygeri, were eager to keep embarking on their journey.

After they got their strength back, they continued to limp before stopping at a ridge overlooking the most low-standard city Ian had ever seen in his life, and judging by his friends' facial expressions, they thought the same too.

"It appears *so...so* dilapidated," Alexis noted. "So run-down!" Drake added. "Definitely corrupted," Jarret said, shaking his head like it needed a made-over. "Most-likely been attacked," Joe considered. "Demolished," Ian muttered, and none of his friends heard that.

Ian saw that there was a sign next to a cliff and hurried over to see what it read. Drake and Alexis followed him.

It said:

In honor of Mr. Howard Crack

And Mr. Carter Dent

Crent, founded 1892, designed by Sister
Sarah Sone

"Who the heck are…?" Drake started and paused. "Strangers!" Alexis said indifferently. "Seems like it," Ian agreed.

Ian looked into the distance at the city, wondering what dangers could be lying there. He had already learned well-enough from his visits to Mooda and Terp.

But anyhow, the architecture of the buildings in the urban area were terrible. One office building appeared as if uneven steps were built into its side, giving the impression that every night, a giant would walk up to sleep on it.

"Come on!" yelled Joe somewhere, "let's keep going!" Drake and even Alexis groaned loudly, Ian surprisingly did not.

It was 7:30 by the time they were just outside the city's boundaries.

"I guess we shall enter!" Jarret said awkwardly. Ian really didn't feel good about the place, it was only fairly larger than a town.

"No matter what, we will stick together, right?" Joe questioned them. "Yeah," Drake sort-of agreed. "Just don't let your minds be deceived, ok?" Joe noted. "Got it," they responded. "Think clearly before making a decision, ok?" Joe added. "Sure," they answered. "Good."

$$* * *$$

Although the narrow passageways were gloomy and gray, the Crystal-Recovered Squad walked-on, keeping their darkest fears at bay.

So far, a single person has not been seen, nor were there any lamps shining light on any surface, forcing them to light candles. How long would they stand, shivering?

At last, they stopped exploring the city at an intersection, and Joe whispered, "Let's spend the night here." "Are you kidding me?" Drake and

Jarret cried at the same time, both a tad soft. "It's like a ghost…" Ian started, but froze abruptly.

All around them, real human beings just came into view. But they were all *broken*. Some had snapped-bones without layers of flesh making it invisible, that weren't treated for decades. Others had skin that poked out in unusual angles, and parts that sunk rather deep until touching inside organs.

The thing is, these people didn't have bruises, scars, cuts, and the many types of minor wounds. They had major and nasty ones! No blood, but unpleasant to the naked-eye.

"Z-z-zombies!" Jarret screamed, but didn't make a run for it. It was just all too much to take-in. Were they doomed?

"Allow me to introduce myself," came a solid voice. A man with zero infections and zero *broken* areas on his body stepped out of the gray.

Ian and his friends couldn't speak, couldn't talk, or at least blurt some phrase or word out. Nothing occurred to them but to just wish they were relaxing on a private beach instead.

"Those who ever set foot here are required to get hurt in a painful way," the unknown man announced. "Our best offer is getting an anvil dropped on you," he said, pointing at a dude who had a smudged head between his shoulders.

"And please remember," he spoke, his expression turning dark, "we are not zombies!" "Oh," Jarret squeaked, really softly.

"Come, let me take you to the Deciding Space," the man offered. "What if we…" Alexis started, gathering the urge to speak.

"Refuse? If you do, the results will be ugly, so please…do not! I wouldn't want to spoil anything for you. Come, let me give you a tour of this paradise!" the man ordered, a tad strict.

They were outnumbered, so checking-out what the cryptic man wanted to show them was a better idea than attempting to head-on escape.

Ian started formally marching like a real guy. Drake reluctantly followed, watching his feet as he strode. Alexis began pacing and gritting her teeth with Blake and Batelo looking extremely freaked-out on her back. Joe's expression was serious with no hint of a grin.

"Um," Jarret cleared his throat, "who are you?" he asked the man. "Carlo Jorge," he replied smoothly. "Then how come…" Jarret started. "You don't have any broken body parts?" Carlo Jorge finished.

"Yeah, that was precisely what I was going to say!" Jarret exclaimed. "How did you read my mind?" "Experience," Carlo Jorge shrugged.

"So…are you mayor of this…?" Drake interrupted. "In a way…yes," Carl Jorge said. "What do you mean?" "It's not necessary to explain." "Why?" "Just forget about it!" Carlo Jorge snapped angrily.

"Ok, fine," Drake rolled his eyes. Ian flashed a glance to see how Carlo would react. Surprisingly, he didn't do anything.

They went-on for about fifteen minutes before halting in front of a concave-quadrilateral-shaped building that rose 30 feet into the air only. It was as large as a football stadium, but with a low ceiling.

"Welcome to City Hall," Carlo Jorge cried. "This is the center of the city?" Ian inquired. "Yup! What are you waiting for? Head in!" Carlo Jorge exclaimed.

Each pillar that rose to the roof like bars were only a foot from each other (Ian had some difficulty slipping through sideways even though he wasn't fat).

Then Ian turned, realizing he was only inches away from a gargantuan door made of shredded sticks.

Thorns stuck out, making Ian grimace. He heard Alexis and Jarret feign surprise. From far-away, the door might have looked furry. Why hadn't they used metal?

"Uh…how are we going to get....?" Joe asked. "In? Watch and learn!" Carlo Jorge exclaimed.

He took out a drill from beneath his oversized-coat. "Wait, wait, wait, won't the alarm start ringing?" Alexis questioned. "In this town, there aren't any," Carlo Jorge replied nonchalantly. "Oh, ok," Alexis muttered back.

Carlo Jorge made a vertical gap in the middle of the door with his drill, and then, taking his gloved-hands, pulled on either side, and broke the door into two. "Walk in, or get destroyed," Carlo Jorge ordered.

Drake, Ian, and Joe went in as Carlo Jorge cried outside, "No need to accompany me, I will be okay. I can handle myself, no need for bodyguards."

Several seconds later, Alexis and Jarret entered City Hall.

Ian's eyes studied the room closely, he didn't expect much. It did resemble a king's palace, but without a throne and banners strapped to the wall. The ground was made of smooth stone, which was good.

A minute later, Carlo Jorge came in with a serious countenance. "Hurry, we need a plan," he whispered silently to them. "What?" Jarret inquired.

"Just get me a paper and a pen right now, they are only giving me fifteen minutes, hustle!" Carlo Jorge spoke swiftly, with an apprehensive expression, pointing to a shelf in the corner.

In less than thirty seconds, the materials were on the table, in front of the man.

He heaved a sigh of relief and said, "I always resented this ugly town…no, I mean city. We need to escape, and I guarantee you, it will not be easy."

"Huh? Aren't you one of *them*?" Ian blurted. "I thought I was, but not anymore. Listen, I will elaborate later, please…it has already been a minute!" Carlo Jorge cried anxiously.

For a tedious eight minutes, they created a simple plan.

A part was like, "They have devices around the streets that detect sound from your footsteps," Carlo Jorge said. "We can tiptoe," Drake considered. "It doesn't work," Carlo Jorge shook his head. "What?" Drake responded.

✳ ✳ ✳

In the night's natural darkness, six people ran and hid from time-to-time. Each of their shoes had leather wrapped around them to reduce the noise.

After shifting around for some-time, they rested under a needed-repair lamppost.

Twelve minutes had passed since leaving City Hall. They could hear *broken* people howling in frustration and anguish.

"What now?" Alexis asked. "We keep going! What do you mean?" Drake said. "Come on, let's resume our pleasant stroll," Carlo Jorge urged sarcastically. Joe eyed him warily. Both Ian and Jarret nodded agreement.

They continue to pass through blocks before turning a corner and almost stepping on puddles with chewed-gum at the bottom. Voices erupted from somewhere nearby. Traps were laid.

"I'm scared," Jarret whispered. "What?" Ian whispered back. "I thought…"

"No, really, seriously, I may seem tough sometimes, but hey, I'm still seven, you can't blame me," Jarret explained vigorously, taking deep breaths between words. Joe nudged him and said, "Quiet!"

They scrambled up and sprinted silently to the opposite sidewalk, across the street. Alexis and Carlo peered through windows, making sure they weren't stalked or tail-backed.

After another five minutes, they saw the edge of the city in clear view.

Then, suddenly, Blake and Batelo the Moygeri both yelped so loud that it was nearly like a scream.

Ian wisped all the way around, seeing a leak in a drainage pipe with brown liquid dripping out of it onto thick chunks of wood with orange flickering on them. Fire. There was going to be an explosion.

"Jump everybody, jump!" Joe ordered. For a moment, Ian didn't know if he should run or hop. He was sweating bullets and wanted to be indoors. Why couldn't he just stand there?

Ian jumped anyway, but accidentally with his head facing the wrong way.

The blast was hard and extremely *warm.* Ian, for some reason, didn't shut his eyes. He watched, his eyes starting to swell with tears rolling out of the sockets.

The scene was beautiful. Bits of brown polka-dots flying in an aura of yellow and red in a starry night sky made it look ethereal, too attractive to the naked-eye.

The flames were about to engulf him when an arm reached-out and grabbed his shoulder. Ian Lanterncup flung into the air, then went SMACK with his back onto a soft foundation.

He suddenly felt unusually lethargic, his head rocking back and forth. Then Ian dozed off, again.

Six: The Only Chaperone

"Is he dead?" Drake asked calmly. "NO! What kind of a best-friend are you?" Alexis questioned with disbelief.

"We definitely can't take him to a public area," Joe pointed out. "Yup," Jarret agreed.

"Would someone go into a pharmacy and get topical ointments for him?" Carlo Jorge said. "Anyone volunteer?" he asked.

Ian became conscious again, feeling that he was on a furry bed that was hovering in the air. His eyes flew-open, and realized that Blake the Moygeri was carrying him.

"What in the world?" Ian grimaced and rolled off his arms. He landed on rocky ground, his back aching. Ian groaned.

"What a surprise!" Carlo and Joe exclaimed at the same time. Ian gasped for breath.

"Where...are...we?" Ian inquired in short breaths. "Not a city," Jarret noted. "So, the wilderness?" Ian asked, already knowing he was right. "Yes," Drake corroborated.

Ian got-up, and limped to a nearby stream. He knelt and drank straight into his mouth.

After Ian washed his face, he stood up, turned around, and cried, "I hate to say…in the future, if I become head of the military base IITC, I will order drones to drop dozens of nukes on that…that ghost-city!"

"Sure, why not?" Drake, Jarret and even Alexis spoke back at the same time.

"Listen…kids, we are going to head to a wasteland south of here to spend tomorrow night there, it is a good and covert place to," Carlo said.

"What? Why can't somebody keep watch as others sleep in a forest or something?" Joe questioned him.

"Common sense number one, whoever does that will fall asleep any moment during their time on duty, because they are really tired," Carlo explained.

"We can call Flix!" Alexis exclaimed. "Who…? Carlo started. "A friends of ours that never sleeps," Alexis replied nonchalantly. "He is a Shadow Clan citizen," she added. "Oh!" Carlo rubbed the back of his head.

"Ian, do you still have that Shadow-Talk of yours?" Drake asked. "Let us see it," he added. "I think so," Ian answered.

Ian put his left hand in his pocket and tugged at anything that could be in there. Nothing. "How?" Ian unintentionally blurted, a tad loud. "What?" Alexis asked willingly. "It's not here!" Ian exclaimed.

"The device must have fell out of your pocket when you flew into the air after the explosion," Jarret considered. "That's not good," Joe said. "Are you kidding me? That's terrible! We've just lost contact with Flix, and plus, his support," Alexis cried.

"I'm hungry," Ian interrupted. "Me too," Jarret pointed his thumb at himself. "Me three," Drake nodded his head desperately. "You boys are driving me crazy!" Alexis yelled.

So they ate their packed-crunchy-bread sandwiches. The turkey and the lettuce were outdated, so they only ate the bread covered with mayonnaise.

Before long, all the cold snacks in their duffel bags were gone and in stomachs. They would have to buy food for their next meal.

So Ian, Alexis, Drake, Jarret, Carlo, Joe, and the two Moygeri walked-on, before finally stopping to rest for the remaining of the night. It was already 1:20 am.

Morning arrived quickly, and Ian Lanterncup was forced to wake up because the sun wouldn't bother to stop shining.

Jarret was ordered to sleep in the same tent as him, so Ian had to be extra mindful with how much noise he caused in the process of trying to get outside. He was successful in not making the snoring cease.

Ian unzipped the flaps and wormed into the outdoors. He put on his lace-less sport-shoes, and was in the process of lifting himself to full-height when he heard shouting. Ian froze.

"His own mother told me I should be the only adult with them on this…" came the angry voice of Joe.

"She definitely didn't particularly mean that!" Carlo Jorge squeaked.

"Oh yes, she did!" Joe replied. "I don't think…" "Take it to heart!" Joe cried. "No way, I can't assume that…" Carlo started, but somehow shut his mouth instantly.

Ian risked a peer. He saw that Joe had a pointed-stick to Carlo Jorge's throat. It was a very unusual sight.

"Ok," Carlo Jorge said, "just one thing I want to make sure, is that, are you jealous of me because of something?"

"You act too smart and cool in front of those kids, and later-on, they will dump me into a dust-bin, even though I don't fit in one," Joe responded, with a tad remorse.

Carlo gave a hearty laugh. "Of course they won't, you seriously think so?" Carlo answered. "Yes," Joe replied smoothly. "Oh well, you will see," Carlo noted.

"Not so fast!" Joe announced automatically. "What? Why?" Carlo asked. "I'm not done with you," Joe spoke. "Come on, it's not a big deal," Carlo pointed out. "To me it is," Joe said. "Calm yourself down, that will make you feel better," Carlo winked.

"I can't!" Joe screamed. "Of course you can, nothing's impossible that deals with emotions," Carlo blurted vigorously.

"Now…if you excuse me," Carlo started. "Stay where you are! Help me carry the burden by doing so!" Joe cried.

Then Ian saw Drake and Alexis run at them with hands ready to push and pull. They did what they needed to, and everyone was silent.

Seven: The Wasteland of Hardships

"Can we please stop at Lotan?" Jarret inquired after a yawn and neck-stretch. "Why?" Ian asked back. "Because I want ice cream! The temperature here isn't cool enough as it was back in Yart," Jarret complained.

The altercation involving Joe and Carlo had long-passed as they continued going south towards a wasteland they were sort-of ordered to arrive at as a destination for the night.

Anyway, there was still an air of uneasiness, and both kept distances from each other, Ian realized after 45 minutes of walking.

"Why can't we just go to a nearby farm, abduct a few horse, taking a carriage during the process, and tie it to the mules so that they would transport us instead?" Drake said.

"Of course not, that is *illegal,* plus, not even knowing how to ride one is the real problem! I am very sure and hope you already know!" Alexis admonished him. Drake kept quiet.

Before they knew it, it was 12:00. "What's for lunch?" Ian asked. "We are going to skip this meal," Carlo spoke suddenly. Joe gaped at him, but snorted instead of talking-back.

"But I'm, I am…" Drake paused for a moment. "I know it starts with an H…" "Hungry?" Alexis raised an eyebrow. "Oh yeah, that's it," Drake responded. "Now I remember."

Along the way, Batelo the Moygeri found a wagon with only one wheel attached to it in a ditch, lying at the bottom.

She'd hopped into it, and instantly, her arms, legs, and belly became red, which was the color of the wagon.

Joe insisted they kept it where it was, but Alexis and Jarret refused.

So to prevent another altercation, they held a vote. It was all-to-one, which made him pretty angry.

Anyhow, Joe was rather sheepish afterwards as Carlo stood in the background with no sound coming-out of his mouth.

Right before dusk, they saw that, in the distance, were endless miles of irregular-shaped mounds of piled-up no-needs.

"This paradise is where we are going to spend the night?" Ian questioned. "Yup!" Drake substantiated. "Well, at least I think very so," he added.

They dragged themselves toward the lonely and deserted place (except for some cats and rats) that was, in a way, creepy.

As Ian got closer, he couldn't smell fresh air, but was instead, replaced by the strong stench of dirty undies that could only be rewashed with bleach, and rotting carcasses.

"I abhor this place! How big is this…?" Alexis shut her eyes and started breathing with her mouth instead of her nose.

"Well, it sits next to the Forbidden Landscape, so I have no idea," Carlo whispered to her. Unfortunately, Joe heard that.

"Hey!" Joe cried like he was caught robbing something valuable from a shelf. Carlo abruptly made several gestures at once and froze. "That's not nice, Joe, he was telling me something unimportant!" Alexis noted.

Joe mouthed to Carlo, "See? They are starting to detest me!" But Carlo knew better than to speak-back or watch his mouth-movements, so therefore, ignored him.

The wasteland had anything you could have dreamed for that was not made-up. Ian knew better than to touch anything there, but his cousin, not so much.

Ian had to remind Jarret over and over again that if one of the mounds lost stability, it would break-apart and all the trash would slide down and cover more area than before.

There was a box of ripped-open cheerios that must have once been yellowish-white, but now gray with a tinge of brown. Ian almost puked at the sight of it.

They went deeper into the wasteland, having second thoughts about the place they were planning to spend the night in.

Their hopes and doubts were like competitors trying to outnumber each other. Except, the game wasn't going to end as long as they were technically in the wasteland.

Drake tried to act like he wasn't afraid with their surroundings, but Ian knew he had at least a tad fear smoldering in him.

Suddenly, Ian couldn't concentrate. He heard voices from the void.

"Give me a dollar! I'm broke!" a woman spoke. "No please…I have nothing!" a man exclaimed, and he screamed. "Seriously! I'm a beggar too, no, don't…ah!" his last words were. "Now…who's my next victim?" she asked to herself greedily.

"Is father coming?" a kid asked. "He…he is ok, the soldiers came, and your dad is just…just lifeless in the garage, but we are safe here," his mom said, her lips quivering. "What's that mean?" the kid demanded. "I…I don't know," his mom lied, sobbing really hardly.

"Are we going with mama or papa?" a little girl inquired. "B…both!" her big brother lied melancholy. "But I thought they didn't like each other anymore," the little girl whispered. "Don't say anything…they are next door, you hear them yelling at each other?" big brother spoke. "So…they are going to get rid of us?" the little girl asked. "No! Yes! Just stop!" big brother answered adamantly.

Ian looked at Alexis. Her eyes were shiny. Water was building-up in them. She scratched her cheek to stop the flow, but it was no use. It was almost like her eyes were melting. Alexis didn't dare look-back at Ian.

"This gloomy place makes me miserable and sorry hardship ever existed," Jarret noted. "That is so profound," Ian whispered-back, into his ear. "I wish other could also be like us," Ian added. "So happy, so joyful," Jarret extended.

"It's so depressing!" Alexis cried at once. "Poverty and war and divorce and…" she broke off. "Can we get out of here right now?" Alexis squeaked desperately.

"Sorry, we're lost," Carlo pointed out. "Wait a minute, how come I didn't think of this," Drake muttered. "Think of what?" Ian asked.

Drake looked at Carlo. "You brought us here for another purpose, didn't you? You knew what haunts this place all along!" Carlo bent his lips. "How are you so sure, then?"

"It too obvious!" Alexis interrupted. "I thought you were an extremely smart man that I could count on. But what I also know, is that, the moment we walked into here, the voices distracted us, and somehow, our feet kept moving. My guess is that…you led us to this reclusive place for a rather simple reason."

"What is it?" Joe demanded out of the blue. "Yeah, tell us at this instant!" Jarret ordered. "Come on, don't be shy," Ian said.

Carlo grinned with his mouth ajar. His countenance was murderous. "Haven't you thought earlier?" he questioned. And with a hand in front of him, he announced, "This is me, the new Ziknio of Mooda and Adolko!"

Eight: Driving without a License

"What the…" they all exclaimed. "How is this possible?" Drake asked foolishly. "You were Carlo of…to Ziknio of…how?" Alexis inquired, extremely perplexed. "You were dead a long time ago, well, not really," Ian added.

"Its common sense," Ziknio started. "The guy who fell into that swirly-multi-colored tornado thingamajig was actually my twin!" he explained with clarity. Joe looked as if he'd just gotten bashed in his brain several times.

"Anyway, it's time for slaughtering!" Ziknio exclaimed when nobody responded to his explanation. He took out an exact replica of the same dagger his twin used.

"About your twin…" started Jarret, "did he have his own name or was he also called…." "No more daylight-burning questions!" Ziknio screamed. "It's evening already," Ian pointed out. "Just…" he pinned his weapon into an empty can of canned-beans lying at his feet.

"You see this?" he said. "This will happen to you in a tiny-while, now prepare," Ziknio spoke roughly. Ian knew he had to do something as usual. The chances were low, but it was worth trying.

Ian tapped Joe and Drake on their backs and made heads-up to them. Fortunately, they understood and drew their weapons.

"Oh...you guys want a duel?" Ziknio smiled and looked away. "It's obvious!" Ian cried. "Well, well, well, I never *loved* my twin, but this the best moment to avenge him," Ziknio nodded.

"What about this," Alexis started, "you give us twenty seconds to let us run-free, and after that, it's a combination of hide-and-seek-and-kill," she finished.

Ziknio shrugged like it was no big deal. "This is an enormous place, so I don't think you will be able to escape anyway," he noted. Ziknio took Alexis' hand and shook it.

So the villain started counting and they attempted to run back to where they entered. But it wasn't that easy to retrace your steps.

They decided to split into two: Alexis, Drake, Ian, and the Moygeri on one team; Joe and Jarret on the other.

"It's not fair! I don't want to leave Ian!" Jarret had protested. "It's ok, he's with his friends," Joe said, and pulled him away.

Team #1 strode rather quickly keeping a high alert with their ears and eyes, going this way and that. They created a pattern (or code) of turning: right; left; left; right; left; right; left; left; left; right; right; left; and repeating it all over again.

Team #2 however, wasn't doing too good. Joe had to carry the still-sobbing Jarret like a towel slung over one shoulder.

Ian, Alexis, and Drake started sprinting for some time before spotting a silver and moldy Ferrari lying on a bed of cracked-open vases and cupboards in a slanted-direction. Why would one of the world's most expensive race cars be right there in front of his eyes? Ian thought

"Let's hide in there!" Alexis suggested. "What?" Drake and Ian both exclaimed. "Yeah!" "You sure we can still open from within?" Drake asked. Alexis ignored the question.

Ian went to the Ferrari and examined it. Alexis was on the verge of touching it, but Ian grabbed her wrist.

"Don't…germs and bacteria will cause disease!" "I know that, but it's so tempting!" "For your own good, please do not!" Ian said strictly. She grunted, but then moved-away.

Ian did something most people wouldn't. He smashed the driver's seat door with his Wrist Striker, and the next thing he knew, was getting pinned to the muddy ground. Drake was blinking at him, managing a grin.

"Dude, what was that?" Ian exclaimed. "I-I acted against my perfect-looking will and let my dignity overcome me," Drake answered. "He meant that, the Ferrari is worth kept tidy then trying to break-in," Alexis explained.

"Well…too bad, just shut-out your sense of sight and sound as I give this baby a new style!" Ian sat up and spoke. "No!" Drake cried. But his groan was cut-short when Alexis shook-him away. "Nice," Ian replied. She nodded.

Ian gave the Ferrari several large blows as Alexis watched alongside him. Finally, the door was detached from its hinges.

There were only two seats in the car. Ian guessed that one was for the girl, and the other was for her boyfriend.

And something else more surprising was that, a key was there! Their jaws dropped. How could that be?

"Do you think this race car can accommodate the three of us?" whispered Alexis. "Nope!" Ian said, looking around.

"Hey, but..." came the voice of Drake. "My dear old friend!" Ian interrupted, "Is there a bar you could hang-onto at the top? It's very breezy today! And you could *experience* the wind!" Ian asked and added.

"Yeah!" Drake exclaimed after a few seconds. "There's a bar next to the sun-roof," he called-out. "Really?" Alexis inquired hopefully. "Yes!" Drake replied. Ian had to smile, and when he got home, he would write a letter to the company and tell them...thank you.

"But I want to sit with you guys!" Drake suddenly said. "No can do...it's full down here," Alexis spoke-back smoothly. Ian was about to say the same thing.

So Drake hopped on, and Alexis took the passenger seat as Ian attempted to figure out how to operate the system.

A minute later, the Ferrari came to life and rumbled. "I don't get it, why did *they* put this here?" Alexis inquired. "Don't ask me!" Ian chided. "But it certainly did give us some sort of boost," he added.

"This is perilous, and I don't know if I should let this vehicle run," Ian muttered, inhaling. "Well...it already whirled to life, so why don't you proceed?" Alexis suggested. "You're right," Ian responded.

So Ian Lanterncup, a beginner, and not even an amateur in driving put his heel on the floor and stepped on the pedal. Why did he even start the engine before?

"Ahhhh...ahhhhh!" Ian screamed. He twisted the wheel anyway he insisted in split seconds, dodging piles of trash.

"This is not a very good idea!" Ian cried. "I can't focus on where we are going!" he added. Alexis didn't answer, or maybe she couldn't.

Ian tried to think of euphoric moments when he was young, not nerve-wrenching ones. He looked at Alexis, her eyes were wide open, her hands gripping her chair. "Hold on, it will stop before long," Ian promised her.

Only ten tedious seconds had passed and Ian spotted Ziknio somewhere. He was momentarily distracted, and the Ferrari went crashing into a mound of tinfoil. There was complete pitch-black darkness. "Uh-oh," Ian uttered.

He tried to get the Ferrari to move, but it was severely stuck.

Maybe Ziknio wouldn't want to dig through all that trash to get to them," Ian thought hopefully. But he couldn't stay where he was.

Ian wished he brought a cell phone with him so he could call Joe to come and save them, but was there even internet connection there?

Then, there was a loud POUND, POUND, POUND, and Ian had to take a moment to realize that Drake was causing the sound from atop. Ian saw his face through the sun-roof. Ian shuddered, not wanting to imagine how Drake felt under all that stinky-stuff.

Alexis seemed to recover from her shock and said, "What now?" Ian considered on this. "Excuse me?" "You are the boss...so what now?" she asked again.

"Uh...nothing?" Ian replied feebly and shrugged. "Oh, really, huh?" Alexis questioned him. "Yes!" Ian confirmed.

Then there was a squeal, and both of them glanced up, seeing Drake twist and toss uncomfortably. "It must be a mouse in his shirt that is causing that," Alexis smirked. "Yeah," Ian replied, rather politely.

Suddenly, the Ferrari was pushed sideways and natural light *exploded* everywhere. The next thing they knew was seeing a yellow bulldozer appear from within the mound of tinfoil. Ian could see Jarret arching an eyebrow in it. Where in the world did he learn to drive one?

Ian stepped out of the Ferrari, and Alexis did the same on the other side.

They hurried out, and both asked, "Where's Joe?" "Over there," Jarret pointed to thirty-five feet away, where Joe and Ziknio were beating each other to their deaths.

"We need to help…" Ian started. "Wait, just one question for you two…isn't that sort of race car for newly-wed…" Jarret could barely finish the S at the end as Ian cupped his own hand on his cousin's mouth. "Say that one more time, and I will…" "Hey, come on, Ian, don't you care about Joe?" Drake called. Ian snorted and muttered, "Next time," to Jarret.

The three of them were sprinting. Ziknio threw his dagger, the cusp missing Joe by inches. Unfortunately, the edge pierced his cheek, and Joe went tumbling into a little pile of worn-out and chipped ukuleles.

Drake took his place. He brandished his glade and created a whirlwind with it by spinning it non-stop like a fan. Ziknio just shook his head and said, "That's all you got? What a callow method!" Drake replied, "I'm a kid, and kids have creative methods, you get it?" Ziknio grinned again and went charging at him, ready to drive the dagger through him.

Drake knelt intentionally right before Ziknio swung his weapon at the bridge of his nose. But then, the dagger went clean through his hair, and Drake, through a cracked-mirror, saw that he was nearly bald. "What!!!!" Even Ziknio looked surprised, but seconds later, laughed.

"You have an interesting coiffure! You look so hilarious! Hahahahahaha…." Ziknio continued to chuckle, tears spattering onto the muddy ground.

But as he did, Joe went up behind him, and stabbed him with his staff, the 'Lost Crystal of Len' poking out of his chest even though it wasn't *so* pointed. Ziknio blinked twice, paused, and blinked twice once more. "Well, too bad for you guys, because there are many more of me!" he exclaimed.

Ziknio fell on his posterior and ripped the skin of his belly open.

There was no flesh or bones under the peeled-skin, just, and only, metal. Ziknio put his face forward and was calm.

"Oh...that's why," Jarret muttered somewhere. "Ziknio is a type of robot," Jarret explained. "How are you not reluctant?" Ian asked demandingly. "I know this, just trust me, that's all you have to do," Jarret notified him.

"I think he's right," Joe said. "I'm a smart kid that is wise too!" Jarret bragged loudly, giving Ian the evil-eye. "Ok, ok, ok," Ian waved the subject away, "but how are we going to get out of this dump-for-eternity-place?" "Hmm," they all thought.

Nine: No-Good News

How did they find the way out? Joe was fond enough to have put tiny sticks he carried in his pocket on different items on different mounds from where they entered. So, it was an easy job that was well-done.

It was already past sun-down, and Joe volunteered to keep night-watch as they slept. Ian's friends, of course, protested, but Joe *insisted* to, and that was the end of the topic.

As Ian was about to cover himself with his blanket in his tent and on his mattress, Jarret coughed once, and spoke, "I need to tell you something." Ian was rather curious and made a 'continue' gesture with his hand. Jarret nodded.

"Remember when I intentionally jumped off that bridge over the Kiffe River?" Jarret started. "Yeah?" Ian replied, clearing asking for more.

"I think The Haunter had ordered the Zartees to only murder one person, and he thought that the Zartees would understand what he said, that the target was you. But I knew about it all along. So I sacrificed myself so that you would not die. I know what you're thinking now, that you're a horrible cousin, who should've died for me instead. You see?" Jarret explained swiftly.

"Wow," Ian exclaimed, "cuz, you really are smart and wise!" he finished. "I am, and feel deeply flattered," Jarret grinned. "No matter what happens, you are still my…BCF," Ian said.

"There's still one thing that is not clear to me, one thing! And that is, why did I come back to life?" Jarret cried loudly. Ian remained quiet. "Tell me!" Jarret seemingly begged his surroundings. "While you do that, I'm going to sleep," Ian noted. Jarret didn't seem to hear him.

* * *

The next morning, they packed their belongings and started walking again. "We need to eat! Breakfast is crucial!" Drake complained. "Fine, are there any open-businesses nearby?" Joe asked angrily. "Uh-no?" "There you go! Think before you speak next time!"

"So…are we going to have breakfast when we get to Teek?" Ian inquired hopefully. "Of course!" answered Joe. "Why not?" he added.

Ian knew that the two Moygeri were starving for they were digging their black nails into Alexis' shirt as she tried to stop them.

By mid-day, they saw Teek from a distance, lying on flat-land. Ian had learned in school, that, cities on flat-land were constantly flooded. Thank God, the city didn't resemble that ghost...town, Ian thought.

The city was large, and Ian was relieved to see real people on the streets.

Alexis spotted a little building called 'Papa Noigle's Chill with Platter Diner' and with the result of a vote being 3-for; 2-against; they went over the street and into it, through a pair of loose flip-flap doors.

They had an ordinary breakfast. Drake didn't like his eggs, so he offered some to Blake. He munched them up happily. "Drake! Have you ever heard of food poisoning?" Alexis questioned him. "Yes, but its human food, and that's ok!" "Nooo....these two are of a different race, and you simply can't guarantee that!"

After their meal, they obviously paid, and then went-on to browse around the city. The name 'Teek' in general sounds very old-like and barbaric, but the city could be the opposite of your first impression.

And so the Crystal-Recovered Squad moved alongside shops towards northeast. "This is such a typical city, it's too humdrum to live here," Jarret complained. "You seriously want more trouble that can occur with us included?" Joe raised his eyebrow.

Then Ian heard shouting. And as they got closer, he could see a TV half the size of the Empire State Building sitting on a grand staircase leading-up to it. Citizens crowded the bottom, crying angry comments at the TV. Some yelled sanctions.

"Curse their blood!" one senior said. "How are we going to protect ourselves?" a guy asked desperately. "Is this the end?" another questioned. "It must be!" her relative replied. "Too hopeless! Each can kill before their victim even recognizes!" somebody cried. "We need to leave this planet immediately!" a woman cried. "They will come for us anyway!" someone shouted back. "Oh no! Abandon city!" a random person yelled-out. "Save us, or else I *will* die!" a girl cried.

Ian glanced at the TV screen and was momentarily transfixed. Cooc, another city, was in ruins. Steam covered the sunny-sky. Only a few buildings still stood, but were highly-damaged. It was too gloomy to watch.

Ian guessed that Shadow Clan had caused and brought-about such destruction. Shadow Clan always thought too highly of themselves when compared to human beings. It was true that they were stronger, but because they had the ability to do things that mankind cannot doesn't mean they can only *like* themselves.

Ian remembered when Flix told him about several ones, who still liked humans including him. He bent his cheek to honor them, and hoped they got the message.

Then, something spoke into the TV. "Fools, listen to me," a gruff-looking creature with neon sparkling all-over his steel body appeared. "Your prisoners are on an island next to our territory, which is guarded by the Goliather. If any of you dare stand-up to him, go try! Whoever wrote that newspaper…show yourself, or 160 humans die painfully! Now, the deadline is Tuesday, and today is Saturday, why am I even wasting my time with you useless barn-animals?" and he disappeared.

"Was that all true?" Drake and Alexis muttered, partly to themselves. "I don't know," Ian answered honestly. "But I know that we have to get there fast!" Joe noted. "They will kill us right away!" Jarret cried. "Don't say that, just encourage yourself and us," Joe uttered.

"Uh…so Joe, are we going to take a bus to another city, or…" Ian trailed off. "We will have to cross the sea to a different continent with only two cities, because most of it is covered with the wilderness, which is obviously inhabited by wildlife," Joe replied.

"Ok…then, let's go to the coastline and see what options we have!" Alexis suggested. "Can we also stop by the beach?" Jarret asked. Drake just shrugged as if he liked the idea.

They headed towards the edge of Teek, walking the entire width of the city itself, not even stopping to get some frozen yogurt. Finally, the dark-blue water was visible, and seagulls flew all around them.

"Let's rent jet-skis!" Drake cried-out at first glance. "No…you can easily fall-off one," Alexis muttered to him. "I think it's a great idea!" Joe and Jarret said at the same time. Ian knew Alexis wouldn't be able to convince and persuade them to not ride one anymore.

So they strode over to a little area called 'Crazy's Jet-ski Rentals' and Joe paid an aggregated 90.00 for three in an hour. And knowing that they weren't going to return the jet-skis anyway, they steadied themselves and got onto them.

Ian had to once again share with Jarret. Drake and Alexis had a jet-ski all to themselves (with the exception of the Moygeri). Joe got to have a personal one.

"Follow me! We're going southeast!" Joe shouted over the howling wind. "All right," they answered.

They shot out and away from Teek, water lapping their ankles. "This is so cool! Can I drive?" Jarret asked Ian. "No!" Ian responded, rather strictly.

Just as they hit mid-sea, the clouds turned dark-colored, and rain poured on them. Thunder roared, lightning flashed.

"Why don't we just turn-around now?" Alexis inquired desperately. "Yeah, I think we should," Joe replied.

Ian had drips of water all over his face, and he didn't dare take his hands off to wipe it in possibility that he would lose poise. His eyes were almost all-the-way shut.

"But I don't know how to make a U-turn!" Drake cried somewhere. Jarret was grimacing and squeezing his hands to his ears. Ian opened his eyes and looked one last time at the sky. Then he fell into the rapping waves.

Ten: Relaxation

Non-artificial light bursts everywhere. It was so bright that Ian thought he was looking directly at the sun through his closed-eyes.

Ian felt himself lying on some sort of cushion, perhaps the top of a jellyfish. He then felt the water leave him, and was raised lightly into a tree. Branches tickled Ian's skin. The next thing he knew was being on a random bed.

He opened his eyes in alarm, seeing a gentleman and a girl his age right beside him. They had friendly smiles and seemed rather faultless.

"Hi?" Ian said foolishly. "Let me introduce myself…I am Hapoke, and this is my daughter Reeve," he gestured to the young girl, who was exactly as tall as Ian.

Reeve had even and straight strips of hair that fell all the way to her waist. She wore an elegant dress and skirt made of bright-green silk. She couldn't have been mistaken as a weaver. Ian suddenly choked at her appearance.

"Are you thinking that my clothing look hideous?" Reeve questioned smoothly. "No! I-I didn't mean…um, you look really good!" Ian blurted. He found it hard to talk to her, especially in front of her father.

"Ahem," Hapoke coughed, "here's something to remember...whoever sets foot on this island will always be interrogated." "Wait, where am I?" Ian inquired. "Isn't it on the map?" "I've never payed attention." "Well, check when you get out of here." "Ok."

"Reeve...," Hapoke called out loud. "I want you to make our guest feel at home, ok?" Reeve nodded respectfully and he jumped off a few wooden planks at the edge.

"So...Reeve, um, uh, can you explain what happened to me and where my friends are?" Ian asked, rather soft. Reeve slapped him hard on his cheek. "What was that for?" Ian cried. "Next time, speak a tad louder, but now, listen...I will tell you!" she ordered.

"Whenever people like you enter our property without knowing it, we send storms and take them into custody," Reeve explained. "What?" Ian asked. She slapped him harder this time. "Of course you get it!" Reeve cried. "What sort of mind do you even have?" she added. "Just tell me..." Ian started. "About your friends, they are getting transported here," Reeve replied, reading his thought.

"Hey…can you show me around now?" Ian said as he struggled to get out of bed. "Come along," Reeve stood-up.

"First skill you need to learn…is to jump from sixteen feet in the air!" Reeve spoke. "What? That is insane!" Ian exclaimed. "Watch me," she dove and landed on her two feet without hesitation. "Now you try!"

Ian felt wobbly. He hopped and landed, rolling back-and-forth, clutching his feet. Reeve shook her head above him.

"So…" Ian sputtered on the ground, "Are all your structures built on treetops?" Reeve replied, "Just our houses…see for yourself!" she added, waving her hand.

Sure enough, through leaves, Ian saw many cube-like-shaped buildings just above the canopy. They appeared to be glowing.

"Uh…why are those *houses* so bright?" Ian asked thoughtfully. "Because we use stone that attract fireflies and trap them. This is a way to have light instead of using torches," Reeve noted nonchalantly.

"Do you…have a president or something?" Ian inquired. "Nope! We don't even have a government! And that is because everyone here has perfect self-control," Reeve answered like it was obvious.

"That can't be! What about when people argue?" Ian exclaimed. "We don't really care about what happens…but just assume everyone is living a happy life on this island, ok?" Reeve questioned.

"Fine, now can you take me to the shore to see my friends?" Ian asked. Reeve snorted, "You don't want a tour of this impeccable place?" "Uh…no, thank you!" Ian replied nicely. Reeve punched his forehead. "I don't accept affectation in my presence!" she noted. "And please, don't try to be kind and gentle to me!" Ian glanced away, a tad puzzled at what Reeve said.

Reeve was pretty, but too aggressive according to Ian's taste. She did give Ian the cannot-breaths at her sight.

Ian hurried after Reeve to the shoreline. He could see multiple figures advancing towards him. Ian ran past Reeve and saw that they were all calling his name.

"Ian, Ian, Ian, Ian!" and Alexis gave him a big teddy-bear hug. And as she side-glanced, her expression darkened.

"Who-are-you?" she asked Reeve slowly. Ian cried, "A new friend of mines!" "What were you *doing* with him?" she questioned. "Oh, uh, we were just talking!" Ian replied. But before Alexis could say anything else, she was pulled-away by Drake, who was constantly flashing glances at Reeve.

"Ok…you guys' interrogation is at 5:30," she spoke, rather harshly. "In the meantime, do whatever you want…order anything…everything's free!" Reeve exclaimed in a false tone and marched-away.

"That girl…is a hot one!" Drake exclaimed. Ian nodded, but wasn't sure why he did that, maybe because Reeve was just too much for him. Ian looked at the distance, hoping to see her for the second time. Drake seemed as if he was going to sprint after her.

It was a balmy day with winds going this way and that. The sun's heat was at its just-right temperature. Then Ian thought, was it always like this here?

"Well…we have several hours ahead of us before the sun goes-down, so why don't just feel good about this place and go do whatever we want?" Jarret asked.

"Yeah!" Joe agreed without reluctance. "But these inhabitants are strangers! And we know nothing about them!" Alexis noted. "Oh, just feel grateful!" Joe replied.

They split-up. Ian decided that he was going to walk the entire perimeter of the island clockwise. Drake caught-up with him and said that he wanted to come-along too. Ian just shrugged because it was no big deal. Joe, Alexis, and the two Moygeri still clinging onto her back bid their farewells and started walking deeper into the island.

So Ian and Drake headed north, only to stop twenty-four minutes later, panting. They went to a nearby outdoor bar where a guy with shades assisted them.

Ian ordered a Starfruit-Pineapple Extreme Cool Mix Shake, and Drake ordered something like a Coconut-Cherry Smoothie with a peeled mango hanging on the rim.

When Ian asked how much his cost, the employee said zero bucks. Drake thought he was joking, but after getting a fierce look from him, he knew it was true. "They think you're breaking the law if you pay!" Ian explained. "Wow," Drake exclaimed, "I love this place!"

So the two life-long friends clinked their glasses together, and walked-over to where the pinkish-yellow sand met the transparent-blue water.

They sat down, took-off their shoes, burrowed their feet in the stress-removing sand, and looked-out at the horizon. It was when the sky meets the sea is how far your eye-sight goes, both thought.

Not only was the day great under the steaming sun, but Ian could actually feel a gentle breeze dancing in the void.

Everything felt faultless, but yet, something was wrong. This is nonsense, he thought, just enjoy yourself.

Ian staggered-up and went to the retreating and charging water, as if it was licking the sand like it was ice cream.

He kneeled-down, and put the side of his face on the surface of the water. Ian felt like his cheek was brand-new again, like all the pimples magically disappeared. He rubbed his skin against the warm water, smiling, never had he felt this great before.

Ian always knew that he never had enough time to think about himself, what he desired in the future, how to make a fortune.

A family of rainbow fish swam freely into shallow water. Ian stretched-out his hand and to his surprise, one tickled him with its fins. So, he thought, not every creature was that scared of human-beings.

Ian trudged back, seeing Drake asleep. He grinned. Ian sat back-down and sipped his fruit shake.

The taste was indescribable, it was better than any other drink in the whole-wide-world, and couldn't be put into words. Here, I can tell you: the drink was authentically, and really sweet, with just the right amount of sour and saltiness, so little that you could barely taste it.

Ian suddenly felt lethargic, his eyes droopy. He stumbled towards a hammock and collapsed on it before he could fall on the sand, and make a big mess on himself.

Eleven: The Escape

Not everyone gets to fall asleep accidentally on a remote island you have no idea of with white water that looks turquoise and sand only half-yellow.

So…if you ever get waken-up from snoozing in that circumstance, I don't think you would be too pleased with it. And that was what Ian Lanterncup had to deal with.

"Wake up! Get up!" somebody called-out at him as he felt being tossed-around by a hand. Ian took-out his own hand and deflected a blow coming at him. He then grabbed the anonymous person's arm and pushed him away, his eyes still closed and resting.

The guy came-back, and Ian flung at him, grabbed what he thought was his shirt-collar, and yanked him away. "Agh, no, don't!" someone else ordered. It was a familiar voice, Reeve's. How embarrassing was it for a girl your age see you snoozing like a pig?

Ian immediately flashed his eyes open, and seeing that his hammock was moving, hopped down to the ground and readied his Wrist Striker. A few buff guys stared at him.

Reeve was dressed in a combat-suit, so were the other men. "What's happening here?" Ian asked, his Wrist Striker aiming at them. Reeve sighed sideways. "Guess! Or don't!"

Ian looked at her. "Fine, tell me," he said. "We are going to be raided by the Dark Elves, they've just destroyed Teek in the distance," she spoke, her eyes suddenly tearful. "How do you know?" Ian asked randomly. "Oh come on! We have spies!" she cried in disbelief.

"But now," she started saying, "You and your friends are going to our Underground Interrogation Chamber for questioning." "Uh...where?" "Beneath our city...Eeeto!" Reeve exclaimed.

"Oh..." Ian nodded several times. Reeve turned away, "Big boys, resume your strolling." Ian looked-up, and Reeve said, "Follow me if you don't want to be kicked-off this island." "Fair enough," Ian replied.

So they trudged, and Ian, couple times, wanted to tell her something about himself but immediately went muted after she brandished her hand, which had a gauntlet covering it, at him. Ian didn't want to waste precious time where he could flirt with her, but it was no use.

Finally, buildings became visible. Ian thought the city was going to be old-fashion-like, but he was wrong.

All the structures were cubical with only the exception of a tall and triangular one with a bulb at the bottom, resembling an onion. It sat left of the center, where an enormous stucco court-house stood. Seeing that, Ian shuddered as he remembered his visit to one.

The walls of the entire city's buildings were made of golden-brown-colored travertine, and the rooves, made of whitish-gray slate.

"Hey," Reeve snapped, "down there!" She pointed to an opening in the ground, under a low hill. "Keep yourself alive," Reeve kissed him on the cheek and headed towards the city. Ian was profoundly surprised. Why would a girl who treated you terribly, give you a kiss to say bye for an hour or so?

The interrogator was Hapoke, which sort-of surprised Ian. His friends sat next to him as he took his seat. "Ok, let's proceed," Hapoke said. Ian knew he was late.

"I hope you all know the simple rules?" Hapoke asked. They nodded. "Now…we are going to head-up to the top of the tower," Hapoke shook his head at a circular-elevator built into the mud. "What for?" Ian inquired. "Reasons," Hapoke shrugged. Why didn't he give a specific answer? Ian thought suspiciously.

They entered the little compartment and the elevator automatically…elevated! They appeared in the sky, seeing Eeeto from a great height. "I love the view," Alexis muttered. "Yeah, me too," Jarret agreed. They continued to ascend until coming to a halt.

The doors departed, revealing an office room. Chairs with cushions supporting your posterior waited to be sat-on. A table stood there without anything on it. A magnificent study-chair with wheels on the bottom faced-them across the table.

"Sit down!" Hapoke offered. They each took their seats, Ian had the window one. Hapoke obviously sat in the master-one. He coughed and started speaking.

"I know something is up with you people, who else would venture close-enough to this perfect place. You see, this island is prohibited. *Different* humans like you guys are afraid of here, they've never sent explores here. But we're humans too, but bolder, and more courageous to take-over, to claim this island," Hapoke explained with clarity.

"Oh…uh, we didn't know, just was on a mission…" Joe started saying. "What?" Hapoke exclaimed. "What mission? Tell me about it!" he begged. Drake side-glanced at Ian and muttered, "do you think he deserves to know?" "Oh, maybe…he might be helpful!" Ian noted thoughtfully, but reluctantly.

"Sorry, I can't tell you," Joe spoke. "I deeply regret what I just said…but it's personal, and private," Joe added. "Really…you *don't* insist of announcing your secret plans to me? Well, case-closed, I will just have to *break* you guys at the Tip!" Hapoke replied. "Excuse me?" Jarret asked. "Oh…you're going to love it!"

Hapoke led the way to an emergency exit in the back and pushed the door open. High gusts blew-in. "Just climb that ladder to the top and wait for me there!" he cried.

One-by-one, they got-up to there. It took Hapoke some time to get-up himself, he was smirking.

"In our land…we give perfect deaths too," he pointed at what he called the Tip, and it was pretty darn sharp. Then, something hit Ian. Why didn't he think of it earlier?

Ian then looked-down at the city with a tad acrophobia smoldering in him. He saw an ambulance with its lights rolling, a huge marketplace with people bargaining, scratches in the road, and cracks in the buildings. Ian turned to face Hapoke.

"Nothing here is perfect, in fact, nothing in the universe is perfect except God!" Ian exclaimed. "Huh? That makes me angrier!" Hapoke glared at him.

"No one is leaving this area alive!" he spoke smoothly as two buff guys appeared next to him, blocking the way down.

"Oh man," Drake whispered. "This is not a good sign," Alexis noted. "Too perilous to be true...you know, wrestling each other to their deaths on a skyscraper a few-thousand feet up. "Bring it on!" Jarret cried.

The two Moygeri looked as if they wanted to jump-off the building and plunge through the clouds, but were still reluctant. They were hugging Alexis' ankles.

Then, there was a terrifying SNAP, and the world seemed as if tilted at a 45 degree angle. Three quarters of a second later, Ian realized that the *tower* was the only thing tilting, and it was going to hit the ground. Ian suddenly got pulled away.

"Guys...hang-on and slide...!" Joe screamed as he pointed to the other end which appeared at the top, except that it was the section where the bulb met the line that poked through the clouds.

They slid towards the other end, at certain times grabbing the thick slanted pole with their hands and taking them off because of friction. It made their hands feel like being burned.

"Link…arms!" Joe ordered quickly. They did without protest, and trying to not glance down, jumped desperately.

Down they went, down, down, down, down. The wind whistled with a piercing high-pitch noise into their ears. All screamed before impact with a counter in the gift shop.

They groaned. Ian knew they'd jumped at the best timing, by not doing it at a great height. They should be thankful.

Suddenly, a massive thing larger than a redwood tree-trunk crashed into the wall of the gift shop. And before it could smash onto Alexis, Drake shoved her away.

The thing went onto the floor with a *thud,* it was the area they hopped-out of. Ian was quite amazed at what his best friend did that was heroic. Drake grinned, and somehow, didn't brag as he usually did.

"What…was that?!" Joe exclaimed. "Don't ask me!" Ian pointed out. "I don't really want to go outside now," he added. "Why?" Drake and Alexis asked. "I don't like seeing structures in ruins," Ian said, recalling the five-star-hotel they escaped from. "Oh…I see," Jarret nodded.

They recovered for another second or two and walked-into the main lobby where people were being evacuated. Ian was wondering why there was a gift shop in an island tourists never would enter before getting interrupted by a policeman with shorts.

"Leave right-away! The Dark Elves have broken-through our lines of defenses and is besieging this city now! While back-up is coming, hide somewhere!!!" he cried, and ran-away, wailing.

"Let's go check-out how the environment outside is like," Alexis suggested. Ian bent his lip, but remain positive. "Yeah, let's be eye-witnesses and see for ourselves!" Drake turned around and went face-to-face with Reeve. She had a nonchalant countenance. Ian suddenly forgot how to talk and acted cool, and it was the same for Drake.

"We are getting-off this island," she said. "Are you..." Joe started. "We have too," she substantiated. Reeve faced Drake again and spoke smoothly, "You...lead us." Ian was a tad disappointed that he wasn't the chosen one. Jarret gave Drake a thumbs-up.

"But what about your father?" Joe asked her. "Don't blame it on me, he is my foster one, and I resent him as much as you guys might," Reeve looked him in the eye.

"Wow, a girl who doesn't even love her own dad who might, in the future, walk her down the aisle at her wedding? How ludicrous is that??" Ian blurted.

Reeve took her gauntlet and hit him in the side with the smooth part in a flash. Ian regret what he said. Jarret was going to say something else, but he closed his mouth almost immediately. Alexis ignored all this.

They hurried out of the bulb, cacophony coming from all-around. "I know an underground tunnel we can use as an exit," Reeve said. Ok, Ian thought. The rest nodded.

Drake led the way with Reeve flanking him. She pointed to a liquor store several blocks down, where cars were honking angrily at each other. People all around were *literally* sprinting, trying to find hiding places before the cryptic Dark Elves invaded.

But it was too late. A wave of arrows rose into the orange sky of evening. Citizens screamed and yelled. It was just two seconds before the arrows began sailing-down.

Ian, his friends, and Reeve just made within twenty feet of the liquor store before they saw the arrows flying down at them. "Dive through this window here!" she said and demonstrated through a candy-cane store. The glass clanked at the base of the broken window. The others dove too at the same time, Ian particularly watching-out for the sharp edges.

At that moment, many people fell onto the wet streets from previous rain and bled to death. Ian couldn't feel sorrier than sorry for them.

Why did this happen? After that thought, Ian realized he was shedding his own tears, but wiped them away immediately before Reeve glimpsed at him.

"I know right…its melancholic," she whispered to Ian anyway. "Wait…you saw me…" "No…didn't I say I had much experience of reading people's emotions?" Reeve questioned.

The truth was…she didn't say that to him, really, but Ian was afraid to tell her that…so didn't answer at all. He wanted to talk-back, but his tongue felt tied together with his teeth.

They waited for an estimated 55 seconds before stepping-out of the candy-cane store and seeing bodies all over the ground.

Joe told them that they could keep their eyes closed as he guided them. He volunteered, but they refused because they didn't only want Joe to experience the tragedy, but that it was worth for all of them to.

Slowly, they made it to the liquor store when a conch-horn sounded. "They are going to start attacking! Hurry! First, get into the kitchen, go to the pantry, open the secret door, and it will reveal a set of stairs," Reeve explained. "Which door?" Joe asked. She ignored him.

"But what about…" Drake started. "I will catch-up soon after you all have went in," Reeve promised him. Ian felt rather jealous of that exchange of words.

And so the Crystal-Recovered Squad ran through the tunnel with their new ally and comrade Reeve, finally bursting into moonlight. "Boat!

There's a boat there!" Alexis and Jarret both pointed-out it somewhere.

After boarding, they turned-on the motor, and it took them away from the island. It had a false name: the Island of Perfection. Steam billowed into the air.

Reeve broke-down into tears. Ian seriously wanted to ask her why she joined them on their mission, and hadn't stayed behind with people she knew, but wasn't sure if he should. Drake appeared at a loss of words too. Joe sat on a bench, his face downcast. It was the beginning of a new life for Reeve.

Twelve: Without Sight

As night arrived, they all fell asleep, this time Ian himself taking watch as Janitor Joe snored louder than his friends.

Ian was partially scared that an enormous whale would fly-out of the water and cause the boat to capsize. Once or twice, he thought he could hear a dolphin making noises in the distant. Ian desperately wanted for morning to arrive in a snap and warm him up.

At last, daylight shone. "Land ho!" Jarret exclaimed on the deck. Joe took a binocular from his duffel bag, saw through it, and twisted the gear for some-time, seeming like he was searching for treasure from a distant, and was too lazy to do the work on land instead.

"I'm guessing it's benign, but let's go and see what comes our way," Joe spoke encouragingly. "I hope no trouble," Ian yawned. "You're wasting your saliva by saying that," Alexis pointed-out.

They entered a smaller body of water, expecting indigenous people to shoot out of the water and attack them. Instead, something like a cloud of dust was forming, but was thicker.

"I don't like the feeling of this, get *me* out of here!" Jarret cried. "You mean *us,* right?" Reeve asked. "Yeah!" Jarret replied. "Of course!" Drake added.

Reeve narrowed her eyes. Ian looked-away at once before she acted and threw a punch. Drake groaned behind Ian. Joe ignored all this. Jarret had his mouth wide-open.

Then, the scene disappeared behind a 360 degree veil of yellowish-pink.

"What's going on?" Alexis said worriedly. Joe looked confounded. Ian pressed his lips together for the worse.

The two Moygeri who were patrolling the edges were blinking multiple times. Even Reeve seemed as if she wanted to dart-away from where she was, to avoid what was happening or about to occur. The truth was, everybody did. Ian thought Reeve was a brave girl anywhere and anytime, but it turns-out that, maybe not.

Then, a sandstorm started. Ian cupped his hands to his eyes and stumbled to the floor. Everyone else did the same thing.

"I've got…I've got…stuff in my eyes!" Jarret cried somewhere. "Mines are slowly becoming burnt donuts!" Ian called-back.

Suddenly, a voice spoke, a familiar one. Ian recognized it before anyone else. Her nickname was BB, short for Bickering Bewitcher, who had ninja stars as weapons.

Ian knew her right away: Lady Harsh, the mixer of consciousness. Yup, she could make people lose their minds and make a person the victim in front of his or hers' friends, who wouldn't even have a clue. Lady Harsh could make this *seem* that and that *seem* this. No one should underestimate her.

"You…!" Ian bellowed. "Yes, me, I'm so fond of you for remembering me from last time, I thought you had short-term memory!" BB teased. "No…I don't!" Ian cried and got a mouthful of sand in his mouth. He took his left hand and quickly scraped all of it out, spat several times into the water, and gagged.

"Why did you come back to *meet* us?" Ian questioned her. "Oh…I missed you guys, your gang, as the police would say!" BB exclaimed. "Where are you?" Ian demanded. "Why…behind the veil…obviously!" BB answered with disbelief.

"Urgh, I will get you!" Ian cried-back. "Try thinking before you speak, it won't be easy, obviously," BB noted.

"Ok, just answer to…why did you create a sandstorm to blind us?" Alexis questioned Lady Harsh. "Oh…about that, this is to hold you guys here as my captives until the Dark Elves arrive and fetch you peeps," she replied.

"Fine…one thing…how did you not die at the collapse of that restaurant you worked at as a…I don't know…the boss?" Drake asked. "Quick reflexes," BB shrugged. "Nothing much, I just *flew* out of there," she added. "Why don't ask yourself instead?" BB inquired. "Never thought of it," Drake shrugged.

Ian didn't want to be stuck at where they were for as long as the Dark Elves took unto arriving. He knew his friends were thinking the same. Was there a solution to sneak-away and beat the sand? Or was it all utterly hopeless? Ian thought for a moment.

Then…the remedy entered Ian's mind. Ian needed to get to the rear of the boat, and knew before the sandstorm started that, he was at the bow. Ian needed to use his sense of touch now. It wasn't the most accurate, but was better than nothing.

Ian started heading backwards, keeping his hand on the railing. After less than 5 secs, he felt something metal. It was one of the two cleats which are the parts that you can tie a rope on, to prevent the boat from floating-away. Ian continued to slowly shuffle across the starboard, finally reaching the transom.

He felt for the motor, and found it. Ian brandished his Wrist Striker, and pulled, wrenching it out of the stern with his fingers and his palm up. Ian hoped he didn't break the motor.

Then, Ian shoved it into the air, the propeller, the fan, facing the sand in front of him, blowing-out a clear view with sunlight shining in, as if mowing a path in the grass.

He slowly opened his eyes. "Everyone, follow me!" Ian cried. His friends also flipped their eyes open and were amazed and taken aback. "Wha?" Jarret and Joe started. "Come on! We are going swimming!" Ian exclaimed.

He pointed the motor over the boat's edge at the sand-covered water. One-by-one, they dove, not even considering how deep they were about to be in.

Ian wasn't an adept at swimming. After a few free-style strokes, he started doggy-paddling his way to the shore, catching breath heavily. He kept sinking and *bobbing* out of the water multiple times, his eyes soaked. Ian rubbed them severely, also trying to keep afloat.

Ian glanced around for Lady Harsh, but his eyes caught Reeve, and for something like an entire hour, he stared at her.

Reeve swam like an expertise athlete, in a straight line, her long hair flying-up every time she popped-out of the water. He looked ridiculous next to her. Then, Ian was shaken-out of his trance by the same voice he heard earlier. His expression abruptly became angry.

"Well, well, well…nice job!" BB announced. "Thanks," Ian muttered sarcastically, poking his head around to try to see the source. "Where are you?" he demanded.

"Remember the mist outside your house? Yeah, that was The Haunter, obviously. He offered some mist to me…and that is how I hide and *fly* away from trouble!" BB exclaimed. Ian suddenly thought of Arnold, his dad. "Show yourself!" Ian cried, very loudly.

Thirteen: False Desires

"Why? Anyway...I won't!" Lady Harsh noted. "Get out...of the air! You are a coward!" Ian bellowed. "Please forgive me...I am not under some sort of coercion, so why would I?" Lady Harsh asked fondly.

"Stop attempting to be kind, just reveal yourself!" Ian grabbed the air in front of him. "No...I surely cannot! It unfair, me against all of you guys," Lady Harsh said slowly, a tad irritated, like she was giving important information to a child who was in a hurry.

"Oh my goodness, are you one of those who back-down much and avoid competitions?" Ian questioned. "Nope...but" "Then show yourself," Ian exclaimed. "I can sense that this is no competition!" Lady Harsh blurted. "Like it's obvious?" Ian cried-back. "Exactly, you just helped me say something!"

"Ian...let's run now," Alexis whispered into his ear apprehensively. "They are coming," she added. Ian glanced into the distant, seeing dark silhouettes against the horizon. "Oh yes...we better leave," Ian replied.

"Well...see *you* around!" Drake called into the wind. "Please...I want to see your face again!" Ian derided. "That was a hilarious joke," Jarret started laughing hysterically.

For a moment, no voice spoke from the void. "I think we scared her away!" Joe whispered to them. "I don't know about this," Ian pointed out, reaching the shore with his friends, and patting salt off his trousers.

"Let's go," Joe muttered. They stood up and went-away from the beach.

"Wow, I can't believe that woman! She's not even coming after us!" Drake said. "I know right?" Jarret agreed. "Don't be too sure yet," Alexis pointed out. "Come on, we were just in a boys-having-fun time! Of course we didn't mean it," Drake argued. Alexis rolled her eyes to reply. Jarret kept quiet.

"Why is it so hot here?" Ian changed subject and whined. "Don't complain," Joe said-back without facing him. "Oh...but I am in control of my own tongue...so don't teach me what to not..." Ian trailed off, suddenly stopping in his steps.

"Oh now," he groaned. "What?" Reeve looked at him. "Our bags…they are still on the boat!" Ian cried.

Drake shrugged. "It's ok…I still have my glade, and Joe has his staff plus the crystal at the top of it, so no big deal." Ian was shaking his head continually like a programed robot.

"Not good, our supplies, they are all gone!" "Calm down, it's nothing, really," Reeve interrupted, and that got Ian's mouth to go *shut,* biting his lip in the process.

"Ouch!" he exclaimed. "He needs to have some self-control," Jarret whispered to Alexis, who nodded willingly.

Joe gestured to them to keep moving and they did as he ordered. Ian saw that they just entered a savanna of some sort.

As they walked, less and less plant-life seem to linger around. Almost no green was in sight by the time they got to a vast and dry land without an end the human eye can spot.

"Let's head back," Drake thought. No one answered his suggestion, not even Joe, who made most of the decisions, obviously.

Jarret put his hand up but dropped it because he changed his mind about something almost abruptly. Ian somehow knew it was nothing important, or was he wrong?

"We have reached the Land of the Uninhabited," Joe announced formally. "How did you know?" Ian asked. Alexis saved him from being smacked by Joe. "Because he watches the TV much for educational purposes, remember?" Alexis cried swiftly.

"So…uh Joe, by the definition of *uninhabited*, do you mean no living organisms except cells and bacteria exist here?" Drake inquired.

"Animals still do…but only east of this section of land, where lies a jungle," Joe responded. "Is it open to tourists?" Jarret asked. "Nope, apparently," Joe replied.

"But how come?" Drake asked. "No idea." "I thought you watched…" Jarret started. "I'm not omniscient, all right?" Joe told him.

"Fine, but what kind of terrain are we in right now?" Jarret asked. "A desert," Reeve interrupted. "What?" Drake accidentally blurted. "Yup, no doubt!" Reeve exclaimed.

Ian listened to all this half-consciously. He'd never visited or been in a desert, but knew many stories about people trying to survive in one with very few equipment. This was going to be a very *great* experience, he thought sarcastically.

"I need to get something in my tummy," Alexis suddenly said. Even the Moygeri clung to her back were rubbing their tummies ferociously. "Me too, you are right," Joe agreed. "Me three, don't forget!" Ian exclaimed.

Jarret was the first to settle and sit down on a dried-out tree trunk covered with dirt. "Uh…what are we going to…?" Drake trailed off. "Eat? No, we are going to drink!" Alexis pointed out. Reeve nodded behind her.

"I don't get it," Drake glared at them. "Oh man…listen, somebody will volunteer to snap-off the spikes and bisect a cactus, because in it, there is sap, which is liquid like water and nectar combined that you can drink-up, you get it now?" Reeve explained with clarity.

"Yeah, kind-of," Drake shrugged. Reeve glanced-away.

Suddenly, everything turned darkish-gray. Ian was startled. Then he heard chanting from his friends.

"Curve tablet, curve tablet, give me one!" Jarret repeated over and over again. "Hair-color transfiguring machine, hair-color transfiguring machine, send me one!" Alexis cried non-stop. "Sixteen pet rats, sixteen pet rats, I need them!" Drake begged. "Plasma gun, plasma gun, please!" Joe cried.

Only Reeve didn't start chanting. Ian looked at her wearily. "How come you aren't…?" "That was what I was going to ask you!" Reeve smiled. How could she be happy in a peculiar situation like this? Ian thought.

"You know what's happening?" Ian inquired desperately. "Yes, this place makes a few people of a group who enters to keep on blurting things out they really want that isn't true. Nature is controlling us by making us lie through our minds, Ian, it's creepy!" Reeve raised her eyebrows. "Wow," Ian exclaimed.

"Why not manipulate everybody in the group instead?" Ian questioned. "You see…nature wants people to witness the power by having someone present who is actually watching!" Reeve noted quickly.

"So…you are telling me that *they* don't know what is occurring to them?" Ian inquired. "Very true," Reeve replied.

"Is there a way to stop this evil-doing?" Ian asked. "I think so, but I'm still not too sure," Reeve spoke. "Then…what *do* you suspect?" Ian questioned. Reeve didn't say anything, he didn't know why.

Suddenly, there was no more chanting. "Wait, what?" Ian blurted as he turned around. His friends had bright purple eyes. "Oh…oh," Ian had his mouth open, backing-away. Then they spoke simultaneously.

"Take your leave now to the jungle where you shall be challenged. If you refuse, disappear into the ground. Cracks are forming, don't be patient. A deep couple-hundred-mile long chasm will replace this desert once and for all," Ian heard all this.

He knew that his dear and former principal, who was now The Shocker (right-hand man of The Haunter) had announced all that through his friends' mouths.

But why not arrive in person to deliver his speech? Maybe it was because he wanted to avoid a fight and just talk. But how did The Shocker hack their mouths and speak through them? Ian pondered hard.

Then, there was a loud rumble. The ground suddenly appeared like it had just suffered in a long drought and was on the verge of crumbling. Oh no, Ian thought. "Run?" Reeve asked him. "No...sprint!" Ian said-back.

And so the Crystal-Recovered Squad ran for their lives tiringly toward east. Ian easily hopped over line-gaps in the solid ground. He also had to piggy-back Jarret because he wasn't fast enough. Reeve was in the front and led the way. Joe hurried right behind her.

Ian looked at Reeve. "You lied to me!" he said. "Oh...that was just a..." she trailed off. "Guess? No way, you sounded arrogant, how could you, and what trickery are you up to, Haunter Minion?" Ian questioned. "Please, I'm innocent," Reeve begged. "I will be observing you!" Ian cried.

The desert-floor behind them kept-on disappearing into the depths as if getting shot by machine gun bullets and melting-off an enormous iceberg.

How could they still run, or *rather,* you can assume, sprint for another several minutes? Ian thought. Of course, they were losing their system of breathing moderately. Instead, the practice of breathing quickly was done. They needed to rest, and that was for sure.

Ian averted his head to his right, seeing Joe having his tongue stuck-out, partly touching the rim of his lips.

Then, Ian had a brilliant idea: his g-hook. Why not use it now?

"Hey guys, we are going to go hovering!" Ian exclaimed. His friends didn't really understand He knew that because they didn't even look at him to see what his expression was like after he spoke his words.

"I mean…we will make-sure we are…how should I describe…ah, glued to one another and fly away only inches from the ground," Ian explained. "That is such a colloquial way to describe…!" Alexis said.

"Who cares?" "Yeah, you are right…now take-out *whatever* you need and we will start *working*!" Alexis noted. The others gave thumbs-up to say that they agreed too.

Ian took his hand, clenched it to become a fist, and dropped the block on the plate of buttons on his Wrist Striker. He pressed the correct one. A metal-claw burst-out of a gap in the front and shot out in search of a place to get ahold off.

While that occurred, they all grabbed onto each other's arms and tightened their fingers around them. Drake had squealed at Joe because he had long nails on his. Joe was never much of a hygiene-concerned guy.

Finally, Ian tugged on the cord connecting the metal-claw with the gadget to make sure it was tight. He shouted, "This is going to get a tad crazy!" Then, Ian rocked his feet back-and-forth on the ground, kicking dust in the process, and jumped-up with one foot.

The next thing he knew was having wind sweeping into his eyes, making them tearful and watering. "This is so *fun*," Drake exclaimed. "I know, right? A bit perilous, but simply safe!" Reeve said.

Wind hummed against their ears for some time unto *real* trees with sophisticated networks of branches came to view. "Yes!" Jarret exclaimed into the air above Ian.

"I feel like vomiting!" Joe announced out of the blue. "Why?" Alexis asked politely. "Too fast," Joe squeaked.

Ian peeked behind him and saw that both Blake and Batelo the Moygeri had purple throats. What did that mean? Ian thought, suddenly desperate to get-away from them. Was there a chance that they were also going to vomit?

As they neared, Ian cried, "Everyone, jump off before you hit that…" he risked a peek behind, seeing nobody. "What?" and with that, he slammed into a bumpy surface before he could turn his face forward again.

Fourteen: The Army of Animals

It was a tree trunk, one without peeled-off bark with a bumpy texture, like low rolling hills from an insect's perspective. Even worse, Ian flew straight into several webs before impact. So now, spiders could be all-over him.

"Help! Help!" Ian screamed uncomfortably. It was all he could *get-out* of his mouth. Ian felt being pulled-away and dropped on the ground. "Huh?" he blurted.

"Am I damaged? Am I seriously hurt? I need a surgeon!" Ian added, not aware of all the eyes staring blankly at him from above. "Stop hallucinating, it's NO for all of your questions!" Joe pointed out.

Ian touched his cheek, there was only a few drops of blood, nothing needed to be treated. "Are you sure I won't actually need a bandage? Would I bleed to death?" he asked foolishly.

"Stop this nonsense at once, you are making me worried!" Alexis noted. "In fact, every human body has platelets that prevent more and more blood to keep leaking out, so that's a good thing," Reeve added.

"Hey Joe…I don't want to go into…" Jarret didn't even have to finish. "Why not?" "You know…I get claustrophobic in one, it's not spacious, many leaves brushing against your skin! The moss on the trees!" Jarret complained.

"Come on," Joe urged. "But…I can't really *enjoy* a walk in there…what if we get lost…anything could happen…!" Jarret whined. "That's the only way to our destination…well anyway, too bad!" Joe ended the conversation quickly.

"Yo! We are heading in!" Joe yelled to the others. Ian got up with the help of Drake's hand. They entered a shady area with large rocks in the dry-mud as Jarret lagged-behind.

"Watch-out for ticks, cliffs, and poison ivy!" Alexis noted. "You think we are that dumb?" Drake asked. "Yeah? So…maybe?" she replied sarcastically.

After some excessive exercise and progress, they…in a way, collapsed. "I think I won't live another day…oh, oh my back!" Joe shut his eyes with teeth clenched, and his hand massaging his back, trying to assuage the pain and make it cease. "Don't say that!" Alexis pointed out.

It took them some time with the churning noises of crickets outside their tents to sleep that night.

Drake wasn't all-in for it, but volunteered to keep watch for them.

Jarret murmured dreamily as he slept. Ian tried to make-out the constellations through the net on the top of his personal tent, which wasn't true now because he *had* to hold his cousin as a guest. Alexis and Reeve shared one.

Dawn came, and everybody was up.

"I haven't had a shower for two weeks and a day!" Ian exclaimed to Joe. "During *authentic* adventures…meaning not exploring a city, you almost have no chance to bathe at all!" Joe noted. "But we do!" Ian cried. "But would you want to…right out in the open?" Joe asked. "Not…so much," Ian replied.

Joe turned his entire body around. "All right, we are going to keep our journey through this jungle by following a stream going north, ok?" he spoke. "Why do we need to?" Drake inquired sleepily.

"Because it's always the best to be around natural water during traveling! Plus, rushing water is better than stable water in ponds because they aren't so bacteria-tainted," Reeve pointed out. "And that is for sure," Alexis confirmed.

"What you said was one of little common sense you share!" Jarret looked at Joe. "Oh, uh, that wasn't much," he answered. All the others faced Joe too.

"Come on…when you get much attention, don't just stand there and condescend yourself!!" Ian explained. "I'm not!" Joe cried. "Maybe you are!" Alexis glared at him. "The truth lies in his heart," Reeve pointed out.

"Enough!" Joe screamed. They immediately went quiet. "From now on until we get out of this terrain…everybody don't talk!" Joe ordered.

He started walking as Jarret wiggled his whole body and waved-away the air in front of him with both his hands because he thought the gnats were mosquitoes. Jarret seemed like he had gone into a tantrum.

Shafts of sunlight shot through the canopy. Ian always wanted to learn more about different types of leaves, but couldn't keep-track of any. Hummingbirds fluttered around them.

The morning was tough for them because they did not have breakfast. Ian felt himself stumble all-around and a few times, almost fall onto the leave-obscured ground. He was obviously energy-less, and so were his friends.

After a while, he touched his neck and found it sticky. Ian's sweat had dried, but his second layer was still in the process of drying, and his third was going to cover-up the stickiness and become even-stickier itself.

Then suddenly, out of the side-edge of his eye, he thought he saw a flash of skin and bumps in it...muscles. Was it a person?

"Guys, guys, I think somebody is stalking us," Ian muttered to his friends with looking at them.

There weren't any responds, so when he turned only his head to see behind himself, Ian's heart hopped in alarm. His friends weren't there, and cannot be seen anywhere in sight. "What? Why? H...?" Ian was about to say 'how' but froze at another familiar voice.

"Hello...and welcome to one of my favorite places to kill time!" someone spoke with a cracking voice.

"Who…I forgot!" Ian asked. "The Breaker…do you even remember me?" he questioned.

Oh my, Ian thought. Out of all The Haunter's minions, this was the one he wanted to not-meet-again and avoid his entire life. In fact, this wasn't a *minion*. The Breaker was honestly too extraordinary to exist.

Sure…he claimed to be human…but some people might have trouble to believe that…and before they made-up their description of him, they would be already smashed between two RVs with a finger lifting each only. And guess what…that isn't impossible according to a muscular man like The Breaker.

Ian wanted to…but truthfully couldn't make-up a good greeting that would meet The Breaker's standards. So he went with the basics.

"Hey salty-scent-from-hair dude, how's life going with you?" Ian asked nonchalantly. The Breaker didn't seem pleased and stomped a foot on the leaves, resulting in a sink-hole.

"Wow…that… is impressive!" Ian squeaked, backing-away. "Nice…easy there…fella!" he added.

Ian did what he could. He positioned himself and ran like how most skinny humans would. Ian didn't know how much time he still had until his time was up…in other words…until his life would end. I need to hope more, Ian thought.

Up ahead…was unfortunate. Vines crossing over each other like left-over strips of paper had thorns and needles all-over them.

Ian was now…really apprehensive. Trees on either side blocked other ways out that could be short-cuts.

He would have to huff-up his courage like a *real* man and charge through the wall of vines. Ian never tried it, but went straight at it without double checking. "I…can…do…this," he said to himself. Ian went into it. Now…there is no need to describe the pain…because it's not necessary.

Ian broke-through like an extremely-lupine tiger on its two-hind feet. He suddenly saw Alexis in front of him, with only her back visible. "Hey!" Ian cried to try to get her attention. "What happened to the others?" Ian added.

He stopped, inhaled, exhaled, and glanced behind himself. The Breaker wasn't there, or maybe he was. It was an enigma.

"Are you ok?" Alexis asked Ian.

"Yeah…just want to know…where is everybody else? And why did they…including you…disappear in thin air?" he questioned irritably.

"Oh…for Drake, Joe and the others…I don't know, but for me…I smelled salt right-away, and I'm sorry to say that…I didn't tell anyone that I was taking my leave. The others might have tried to follow me and got lost, but I seriously am not sure!" Alexis blurted.

"Wow, I don't know if I should trust you anyway!" Ian glared at her. "Your choice," she replied.

"Ok…we need a plan," Ian started. "How long do you think we have?" Alexis asked. "Maybe less than thirty seconds. I think that…The Breaker can actually cause a tree to collapse in no more than eight hits…or blows," Ian thought. Then there was roaring, and time was up.

"Now…little boy, show me your back!" The Breaker ordered. Ian did as he said and turned around. He was immediately pinned to his chest, or at least he thought so.

Ian tried to poke his head around to find Alexis, but she was gone again. The Breaker held the same mace the last time they met. Was Alexis really going to let himself die in vain? Ian thought.

Out of the green came an enormous stampede of jungle animals including toucans, orangutans, hippos, vampire bats, cobras, tarantulas, snapping turtles, hornets, and many more. Ian was let-go as they all climbed, flew, and jumped onto The Breaker from all angles.

Alexis stood there, smiling. Ian stared at her...she was dazzling. He needed to blink several times before he could glance somewhere else. Ian sat-up and then stood.

"Thank...you," Ian muttered at her. By that time, Alexis looked like she was grinning more then she could have.

"So...how did you...you cause this?" Ian jutted his thumb over his shoulder. "Oh...there's a system, I will explain later. Hey, good news, I found our friends!" she said quickly. "Come...follow me this time!" Alexis exclaimed. Ian looked at her, she was beaming.

They fast-walked to a location where Ian could finally see an end to the jungle. His friends and Reeve were there waiting for them.

"Alexis was awesome!" Ian announced. "Really? Why did she do?" Drake inquired. "Pretty much saved my life," Ian shrugged.

"I will explain later…when we are in a better place," he added. "But I want to know now! I'm impatient as you might understand!" Jarret complained. "Ian's right, we get somewhere better and the story will be sold to you, all right?" Joe ended the conversation.

Fifteen: More Bad-News

They found-out that there was bus service to a city called Motique later that day. Joe had to specifically describe on the phone where they were so that a bus would come and pick them up. One arrived, and as they entered and marched-up the steps, air conditioning blasts their bodies.

The ride was about fifty minutes. When they arrived, a nearby buffet was where they headed to without asking each other first. "But we don't have money!" Drake said to Joe. "Oh…right, uh, search the streets!" he ordered.

Each agreed to meet at the entrance of the buffet after twenty-five minutes.

After the time passed-by, they gathered collected money and had only nine dollars and forty-two cents, which is enough to pay for one customer above nine.

So Joe spoke, "You guys sit outside right here…and I will go in to get some food for myself and an additional for you peeps." They agreed, and he entered the buffet.

After eating, they went-over to where a crowd was blurting random things out, similar to what took place in Teek.

What startled Ian was that another gigantic TV sat above a grand staircase. He could see steam in the screen, and knew that an invasion had occurred. The truth was dropped on him. Shadow Clan caused it. How could they?

This time…a different steel-bodied figure appeared and addressed them. "Lar is down! And this city is next! Those filthy liars in Lar were really unconvincing! That is why…all are slaughtered. We have checked the surroundings of the city, no survivors!" it spoke and disappeared. Then, a different figure appeared.

"Flix!" Alexis cried, a tad loud. Sure enough, it was him in the screen. Many people scratched their heads.

"Ian! Ian! You hear me…my kind will target the Tropical-Fruit Plantation on Thursday…please get here now…I know you and your team can do this, now…" the screen fizzled and blacked-out. "No!" Drake exclaimed. People turned their heads to get a good look at them. Ian suddenly wished he wasn't there.

They hurried to the coastline and got there. "Jet-skis again?" Jarret asked. "Yup…you read my mind!" Joe responded. "Yay! I can feel the wind again!" Ian said in a false-tone.

Chapter Sixteen: Defeat the Giant!!

The second time wasn't that exciting. Unlike sleeping on an island in a hammock with the sun shining on you, this was different.

Jet-skiing required some concentration and much balance. But for dozing-off outdoors on a beach without dirty-yellow sand and murky water lapping it, was an experience that didn't include Ian until a couple days ago.

Thanks to his mom…for what she calls 'a waste of money' to Ian's offer of taking a family trip to Saik to enjoy nature and its beauty. Lorry Lanterncup, his mom, always thought it was *humdrum.*

As quickly as time flew, land was spotted in the distant. "So…Joe, people live over there, am I right?" Drake pointed. "Nope!" Joe replied.

"But how? It's surrounded by populated continents! Wait, is that stretch of land an island or…?" Drake considered. "Also a continent. I also have no idea why no *human* lives on it. I am pretty sure that mankind had explored it before…but for some reason…that's the case," Joe answered.

"That reason won't be something good to listen to," Reeve noted. "Yup…that is *so* true," Alexis agreed.

"Is there a way we can steer the ship around the perimeter of the continent to the other side?" Jarret suddenly questioned. "Why…are you scared of land because it bites?" Joe taunted. "It doesn't," Drake pointed out. "Ahgh, you just broke the joke!" Joe cried.

"No! I was just…just asking for all of us," Jarret drew an oval around his friends plus Ian, "and our safety!" "No-can-do… that *will* take us forever!" Joe responded calmly. "Why not?" Jarret demanded. Joe shrugged, "I told you right now!"

"Oh yeah…but," Jarret started but immediately trailed-off at hearing a loud noise that was like from a grumpy old-man who wore farming clothes. "What was that?" Alexis *and* Reeve exclaimed.

The Moygeri were afraid and hid in the Valuable Container built into the Jet-ski. Whatever the source of the noise was…was anything Ian did not really want to meet.

It seemed to be coming from here and there in the distant. Ian wasn't sure which direction it was coming from. He anticipated that it was a yawn…one that could severely damage your ears in the first place.

"See…listen to me!" Jarret whined. "We *should* avoid going on land and avoid *that* in front of us because the sound *might* be coming from there!" he added. "It's just a possibility, a slim one," Joe pointed out.

"Don't be too sure about what you said!" Jarret warned.

"Fine…you are seven, I am forty-three, what right do you have to order me to do this and that?" Joe asked, a tad annoyed through his tone. "Ok then…let it be! You are in control…happy?" Jarret asked. "Yes," Joe replied smoothly.

The edge of the continent neared rather slowly because it was going to be full-moon at that night, which caused extra-strong waves to *roll* at them. Since jet-skis needed gasoline to operate, it was easier. There was a tad turbulence, but was okay enough to handle.

Ian saw that…the continent didn't have any trees growing on it, and by that, I mean…none. There was just an enormous exposed-cave that didn't lead underground. But the thing is…it was like a piece of sausage that was twisted into something like a churro. The long cave went up and down tall hills which only had grass and aster covering them. The continent was an interesting piece of earth above the crust.

Finally, their vehicles touched solid. Immediately after they hopped-off, things didn't go so well. Every step they took, the ground sank ankle-deep. Ian started to have suspicions. Why would the ground under your feet be so mushy and elastic and moveable? He thought.

"Should we go check-out the cave or not?" Drake inquired. "Uh…sure!" Joe said. "Everybody in for it?" he asked. They nodded reluctantly, Ian in particular.

It took them an hour to get to the opening in the cave. "I don't have a good feeling of…" Jarret hesitated. "Oh…you always don't have good feelings, so why blame this…thin cave? Joe exclaimed, in a false cheerful tone.

And together, the men entered first…followed by the ladies, not knowing what was going to be a significant outcome.

What was all the slimy/sticky liquid? Ian's abrupt thought was. He knew his friends were thinking the same…it was obvious.

The walls had a blackish-color. Ian concluded silently in his mind that it was formed with original quartz.

But where did all this goo come from? He thought. Then Ian thought of gelatin, which almost made him puke.

Before long, light was not visible from behind. "Joe, do you have a candle we can…?" Jarret's lip quivered. "Ay, they were all in my duffel bag," Joe replied sadly. "How are we going to go deeper-in?" Alexis asked.

"Um…use your sense of touch!" Joe pointed out. "Only? If that is the case…it's going to be hard!" Reeve noted.

"Then, before torches were invented…what do you think they did?" Joe rebuked her. "That's why they stayed in an area all their lives until coming up with that…" Reeve trailed-off.

"Idea? People back-then were nomads, that can't be…you liar!" Joe cried, his voice reverberating, bouncing-off the wall on both sides. Ian was about to show that he agreed and nod…but for some purpose…he didn't.

They had stopped in their tracks, each tapping the ground anxiously. "Can we please go back where we came from now?" Alexis begged. "Yeah," Drake suggested.

Before they could make their decision, a terrifying scream came from the depths. Each of them trembled once and FROZE with O-mouths. "What…was that?" Alexis whispered intently, her eyes bulging. "Oh man…" Ian muttered. "I don't know about you guys…but bye-bye!" Reeve turned around and went out-of-sight.

Just when the rest were going to turn-back, a gigantic person dove-over them, almost scraping his back against the ceiling of the cave and landed with a THUD.

He started army-crawling and seemed to be grappling for something…or was it someone? "Hurry…break a hole in the wall, Ian!" Joe ordered.

Ian brandished his Wrist Striker in front of him, and by tracing his finger here and there on the button-plate, he found the disintegration-causing one. Barely pointing at the wall, Ian pressed the button and blasts it to chunks in a split-second. "Good job," Drake gave a thumbs-up. Ian felt euphoric…but it didn't last.

They hurried-out and judging by the sound of enormous footsteps behind them, nothing was going to turn-out right.

As they stopped at a ridge, Ian wisped around and faced whatever was coming their way…a super middle-sized and extremely-tall guy who was more than eighteen feet.

His mouth was moving non-stop, like…uncontrollably. "He's speaking Phoenician," Alexis pointed out.

"How do you know?" Ian asked deliberately.

"Heard it before…my mom used to know the language," she said.

"But it's a dead one…I think," Ian blurted. "I know Phoenician is ancient…but," Alexis suddenly got flung into the sky and landed inches from a cliff.

That shook Ian awake. He took a glimpse-up at the guy's face…and suddenly, it hit him. His name was the Goliather. Shadow Clan had mentioned him keeping prisoners. But where were they anyway? Ian thought. Anyhow, they had to survive first…before searching.

The Goliather held a swinging club without spikes on it. Instead, electricity sparkled on the club's surface. A metal chain was tied and super glued to the thick wooden handle.

Run was a word Ian heard plenty of times. But having the *audacity* to attack a living and *extraordinary* person was different.

Ian did neither, and just stood there. It was probably the worst quick-decision he made out of many. Ian didn't even consider defending. He was too transfixed to.

So when the club swung at him, Ian did all he could do…and that was falling to the ground on his side, squashing several aster.

It wasn't a very heroic act. But what else would he do? Ian didn't *feel* like trying to charge at the giant's feet.

But on the upside, he had friends that cared for him and shouted his name. There wasn't just Drake or Joe…there also was Reeve, who cried his name out from above.

She sounded like she was struggling. Ian suddenly overcame his anxiety, rolled-away to dodge a strike at the ground, and did a good Chinese Getup.

"Drink...on my sweat!" Ian screamed into the air...at the sky. The Goliather looked a tad surprised, but his expression was replaced by a chilling and wicked grin.

Ian ran between the bottom-half of the giant's legs, swiping and punching his ankles this way and that. An advantage of Ian's gadget was that it could be used like a sword too...as long as he put enough force and energy in his hand. Ian went into beast-mode.

"Where...are...your...captives?" Ian demanded. The Goliather grunted and snorted. "What is THAT supposed to mean?" Ian questioned.

The giant lifted his foot and pointed it into the distance. "Where exactly?" Ian demanded once more. He was going to continue to torture the Goliather before he told him.

"Ian? Stop...you are killing him," Alexis stood and said. "Excuse me?" Ian asked, taking a break to shake his hand continuously in the air. "Oh no...fall back!" she abruptly yelled. "What? Huh?" Then Ian flew backwards for a few tedious seconds before hitting grass again...or at least he thought so.

Ian slowly recovered from an ache in his gut which was caused by the awkward way his body was when he landed. Finally, Ian stood-up and to his surprise…*typical* human beings were on an island the size of an average living room. But why were they just doing nothing there?

Ian called-out to them. "Hey! Are you guys stranded?" The people saw him and suddenly, brightened. They pointed at him and made happy comments to each other. "Yay! Someone has come to save us! I thought our lives were already destroyed!" somebody exclaimed.

Ian looked around and saw that a ring of water surrounded the tiny island. From the center to the other side where Ian was, the water occupied ten feet across. Maybe something stirred in it, he thought and walked-over to see for himself.

Transparent jellyfish swam freely and undisturbed in every section of the ring as the people on the island shouted sanctions about the Goliather and Shadow Clan.

Ian shuddered. He grinded his teeth. Ian started contemplating on how to save them. Surely…the people on the other side were the captives.

Ian needed to be creative if he was going to help them. There wasn't a boat…so that was a must. What am I going to do? Ian thought, slapping his own forehead over and over again. It was a dumb habit, but he didn't care.

Then, an idea lingered to him. Why didn't he think of the bubble-technique earlier? It wasn't really a creative one, but that didn't matter to him. Ian once used it to escape getting squashed by an out-of-control airplane.

"I've got it!" Ian exclaimed. The people whistled and suddenly became fanatic…cheering for him.

Ian's first step succeeded. He launched-out his hook towards the island. Over the water it soared…and as it went at the ground…a man with a brown-colored torn shirt and wrinkled skin jumped into the air, grabbed the hook, and nailed it into the bottom-side of a tree-trunk. Everyone else enthusiastically cried for him too.

Ian intentionally lifted his feet off the earth and he went flying. "Get outta the way!" he quickly ordered, a tad nervous.

Ian huffed-up air and got a good picture of the tree-trunk he was heading to. Ian wasn't going to repeat the same mistake again. He hopped just before impact.

Ian glanced around and saw that there were precisely twelve captives. "Get into groups of four!" he spoke.

They did as he commanded, and Ian got four bubbles in front of him. "On a count of five, each group will walk into one, all right?" Ian explained with hand-gesture.

He started the countdown and right after the captives got into three of them…Ian touched the first bubble that was created and said, "Take them to Moor, please!"

Ian strode into his own one and said, "Release me the second time I say 'you can' I said it once already!" he added.

✳ ✳ ✳

From high-above, Ian saw that his friends weren't doing so well against the Goliather. He desperately wanted to immediately go and attack him. But by just plunging from that altitude in the air would kill him.

Ian needed to descend closer…as close as possible. He planned an independent surprise attack, but that would require not letting the Goliather realize where he was before striking at him alone.

Finally, Ian signaled with his mouth for the bubble to pop…and it did.

As soon as he was on his two feet again, Ian went in a long circle around the Goliather and fired at the giant with haywire-blasting. It was actually a good button to press in times of skirmishes or battles.

That nonetheless weakened the Goliather so that he had to stumble to his knees.

Drake came behind the giant and stabbed him in the back of his thigh so that he howled. Joe wacked his staff on his head like he was a bad-boy. Jarret tried to be cool by kicking his waist. Blake and Batelo were scratching his face up, leaving deep scars.

The Goliather finally gave-himself-up and face-planted on the grass. "Should we just leave it here to rot?" Reeve asked Joe. "Yeah, why even consider?" he confirmed and asked.

But then, all the attention went onto Ian. "Man...elaborate please," Drake ordered kindly. So Ian told them about literally everything, and at the end, they were utterly amazed. "Wow..." they all exclaimed at the same time. "That was easy for you," Jarret told him.

Seventeen: Concerns & Reflection

Drake, Alexis, and Jarret chatted happily to Ian about what happened when he was gone. Alexis explained that she were extremely worried and thought Ian was dead. Drake said that he wanted to avenge him.

But Jarret's testimony hit Ian the most. His own cousin talked-about how he believed Ian was still alive and healthy with confidence bursting in his chest, which sent Ian into a period of hysteric laughter and a state of euphoria.

After so and so...Ian hugged Jarret and he immediately rebuked his act. "Get off me! I was just..." "Joking? No way...that's impossible," Ian pointed out. Joe laughed along. Reeve stayed rather away somehow.

They headed to where the water met land. "Hey! I see plastic canoes we can *borrow*!" Alexis exclaimed. "Oh...where...found them!" Drake nodded his head. "Are there...?" Ian asked. "Paddles? Yes," Alexis replied.

Before you know it, they were back on the sea, the waves making their canoes sway pleasantly on the water. Everything felt impeccable...but yet, something will always be wrong, Ian had learned.

A gentle breeze was present…which made Ian start thinking.

Soon, they were going to be in the Shadow Clan Territory, which no living human has ever had any knowledge of. In a way…traveling to a foreign land with a different culture you haven't learned about anywhere is scary.

Setting foot on exotic land should be exciting, but the things is…Ian wasn't sure if they could even get-out with their lives…mostly not. Anyway, he had a blessed childhood and almost a year of being a teen. He should be thankful for his supporting friends too.

Ian knew every mistake he made was meant to happen…and though one could make you think you've ruined your own life, it is ok, and nothing to cry about.

Everybody's future is predestined, and each will go differently.

Just remember that, whatever happens…think of any good thing that would possibly come out of a situation or circumstance, and that would cheer you up…I hope.

Ian knew all this…he truly did. All was dark now, with the exception of blue lights dancing in the distance. Any outcome could occur.

Acknowledgements

This time…I wouldn't want to thank people, I want to thank my trips to a couple places which supported me in this book.

I know you might think I'm weird…but hey, sometimes people are eccentric…so take my word and don't try to underestimate your relatives or friends. Do me a favor…don't tell anyone about what I just told you.

First-off, my vacation to Bermuda gave me the opportunity to explore authentic beaches that were actually clean…and they were…*flamboyant.* So while I wrote chapter ten, I imagined myself in that scenery with the help of my visit…of how great I felt when I was there.

Next-off, as I went sight-seeing in Toronto, the CN tower caught my eye. So in chapter eleven, I switched the tower up. I highly recommend you to go and see it yourself in Canada. If you have, compare it with the structure in chapter eleven and jot-down what I'd changed.

Lastly, God is the one to generously thank because of his grace towards me. Whenever I run out of ideas, I pray, and a fresh idea pops into my head the very next day!!!

www.ingramcontent.com/pod-product-compliance
Lightning Source LLC
Chambersburg PA
CBHW051828170626
46807CB00003B/1077